"Understated and elegant. . . . *FOLLY* is delicate like a fine piece of lace, a complication of threads producing a work of simple beauty."

—New York *Daily News*

"In *FOLLY,* Minot again proves herself among the most graceful and gifted of America's up-and-coming authors. She is blessed with the skill of imparting a clear message while weaving a spellbinding story. . . ."

—*Milwaukee Journal*

"Powerful fiction and social commentary. . . . intense and richly complex. . . . Reading *FOLLY* is like hearing distant music. The reader who listens carefully will hear and feel the elegant nuances that underscore what seems at first to be a simple melody."

—*Chicago Sun-Times*

"Minot evokes the era expertly. . . . She uses spare prose with gemlike precision and a painter's eye. . . . *FOLLY* shows its young author to be a master already."

—*Detroit News*

"The cast of characters is large, the plot elaborate. . . . inexorably, we're drawn into the story, and by the time Lilian is on her way to tea at Dolly Cushing's, we've forgotten that *FOLLY* is a historical novel, just as a great play makes us forget we're in the theatre. . . . Minot has extended her wings and . . . the book flies."

—*Vogue*

ACCLAIM FOR SUSAN MINOT'S
FOLLY

"*FOLLY* creeps up on a reader, becoming oddly and unexpectedly affecting. It is also, with all its sly touches of humor, quite sad—not depressing, but laced with melancholy. . . ."

— *The Wall Street Journal*

"Exquisitely crafted. . . . Minot's eye for the acute detail is flawless, period flavor is impeccable, character is drawn with conciseness, and style is repeatedly lovely. . . . Poignantly moving. . . . [and] rich with pleasures from start to finish."

— *Kirkus Reviews*

"Displays a brilliant gift for loading frugal prose with emotion and innuendo. Minot's terse purity of voice achieves a canny, ironic distancing, yet seductively engages the reader in her heroine's quandary."

— *Publishers Weekly*

"At once beautifully crafted and poignantly real. . . . *FOLLY* is a keen examination of one woman's life with its choices and their consequences."

— *Virginia Pilot and Ledger-Star*

"The Edith Wharton comparisons are inevitable, but for all its period flourishes, *FOLLY* is spare and modern, with a certain pessimism of heart that comes with knowing what life is like. . . . Minot's ear has perfect pitch."

— *Allure*

ACCLAIM FOR SUSAN MINOT'S
FOLLY

"Minot's prose is polished and confident, occasionally flashing with small gems. . . . The reader is instantly drawn in."

— *Philadelphia Inquirer*

"The most striking aspect of Minot's writing—her meticulous, pared-down prose—works perfectly with the period atmosphere."

— *Los Angeles Reader*

"Minot writes thoughtful, graceful prose taut with emotion, as if each sentence were a stem holding a flower slightly too big for it."

— *The Commercial Appeal* (Memphis)

"Minot has the gift of being both spare and wholly indulgent; she's full of quiet flourishes . . . Her language is a continuous event. . . ."

— *Village Voice Literary Supplement*

"Minot writes a deft prose. . . . *FOLLY* sustains a mood of surface calm, stretched taut over the real despair of accumulated loss."

— *Kansas City Star*

"Minot is a writer of great charm, empathy, and awareness. . . . [The] precise poised prose is almost stately, recalling the fine art of Edith Wharton and Kate Chopin, but with a wholly original spin and keenness."

— *Booklist*

Books by Susan Minot

Monkeys
Lust & Other Stories
Folly

FOLLY

SUSAN MINOT

WASHINGTON SQUARE PRESS
PUBLISHED BY POCKET BOOKS
New York   London   Toronto   Sydney   Tokyo   Singapore

For Nancy Lemann

Portions of this book appeared originally in the *New England Review*.

This book is a work of fiction. Names, characters, places, and incidents are either the product of the author's imagination or are used fictitiously. Any resemblance to actual events or locales or persons, living or dead, is entirely coincidental.

WSP

A Washington Square Press Publication of
POCKET BOOKS, a division of Simon & Schuster Inc.
1230 Avenue of the Americas, New York, NY 10020

Copyright © 1992 by Susan Minot
Cover design by John Gall
Front cover photo by Jim Douglas

Published by arrangement with Houghton Mifflin Company

Library of Congress Cataloging-in-Publication Data

Minot, Susan.
Folly / Susan Minot.
   p.   cm.
ISBN 0-671-74951-X
I. Title.
PS3563.14755F65   1992
813'.54—dc20   92-21035   CIP

First Washington Square Press trade paperback printing June 1994

10 9 8 7 6 5 4 3 2 1

WASHINGTON SQUARE PRESS and colophon are registered trademarks of Simon & Schuster Inc.

Printed in the U.S.A.

Man is so necessarily foolish that not to be
a fool is merely a varied freak of folly.

BLAISE PASCAL

I

Mr. Eliot

I'M AFRAID there's been a change of plan, Mr. Eliot said. He stood in the dining room where Lilian was having her breakfast and reading a book. Her father had completed his breakfast some time before, having risen as usual at dawn. There are to be no guests at dinner tonight.

Lilian looked up, marking her place with a knife. Why not?

Because I was not informed.

But Ma told you Saturday that Walter Vail was coming. Remember, when you got home.

I said there will be no guests. Mr. Eliot lowered his chin and the light caught his rimless glasses, making them go white.

But he's expecting to come. I've already asked him.

I have said all I am going to say. Mr. Eliot cleared his throat. So we'll see you, just you, this evening. He turned his shoulders toward the door without moving his feet.

I'll think about it, said Lilian in a very small voice.

Mr. Eliot's feet moved. Then we won't expect you, he said and departed the room, leaving her quite alone.

Immediately Lilian sent off a note to Walter Vail saying she was being forced to withdraw her invitation for dinner that evening, making no mystery about who was to blame. Then she found herself suggesting that Walter Vail come anyway, after dinner, after her parents had retired. Lilian was eighteen years old and had never had a rendezvous before, at least not one she had instigated. But everything was different now with the war and she felt different along with it.

His answer came that afternoon and she thrilled to see the handwriting.

Shall I wear a black cloak? Do I climb a trellis? Tell me when and I'll be there.

Yours,
Walter Vail

She composed her reply a number of times, trying for the right tone. She was first cordial then businesslike. She imitated his comic tone then tried for something offhand, anything but being as serious as she felt. She thought of the time she'd met Jimmie Weld on the second green the summer before, and how different this was. She hardly knew what had come over her.

She finally settled on something.

They go up at 9:00. Come to the back garden and I'll let you in at 9:30.

Your accomplice,
Lilian Eliot

That morning while Mr. Eliot was leaving for the office, out in the hall where Lilian could hear, Mrs. Eliot had said,

Edward, but the young man is going off to fight. Is now the time to be so strict?

I didn't like the look of him, Mr. Eliot said getting into his topcoat.

Whatever do you mean?

I've met his father. Mr. Eliot's voice had taken on the rich tones of judgment. The man is a fool, and probably not honorable on top of it.

But this is his son. Mrs. Eliot had sounded weak.

The son takes the look from the father, Mr. Eliot said. He has the same look about him.

It was the most preposterous thing Lilian had ever heard.

THAT AFTERNOON she went to tea at Dolly Cushing's. Lilian's best friend had always been Jane Olney, stern Jane who had the kindest heart she knew, but Jane was in Florida with her family. Besides, Jane was not as interested in boys as Lilian had lately become and so Dolly Cushing's company was more satisfactory.

Dolly Cushing liked nothing better than to flirt. She was the sort of girl who said just what was on her mind whether it offended someone or not. As a young girl Dolly had once locked Lilian in a closet with Dolly's brother Ted who liked Lilian, leaving the two young people silent and mortified staring at the white strip of light while Dolly laughed and stamped out in the hall. Dolly Cushing got away with a lot on account of her looks. She had developed more quickly than the other girls and grew to be like a statue, everything about her larger: great shoulders, mammoth head, wide mouth. It was as if the extra bit which had gone into her physique left that much less for her brain. She maintained a steely positive outlook, remembering only pleasant things, striking the matches for her cigarettes with an optimistic air. She wore her shiny black hair with a clean white part down the middle.

Lilian told her about Walter Vail, trying for the offhand, and Dolly immediately sniffed the intrigue. Her eyes shone.

All right, Dolly said, and resettled herself against the cushions. First things first: he's going away.

Lilian nodded. I wanted to say something to him about —

God no! cried Dolly. You must never let a boy know how you feel. Dolly Cushing was delighted to advise Lilian. Being unofficially engaged to Freddie Vernon, she saw herself as an experienced older woman.

It was familiar to be given advice. Her mother had plenty of it. Always look happy. Always be clean. Don't cross your legs. Thank the host and hostess. Stand up when a grownup enters and leaves a room. Make your own bed. Don't talk back. Don't argue with your brother. Ask to be excused from the table. Never raise your voice. Be punctual. Don't frown.

And there were all the things one wasn't to talk about. One's health. Bodily functions. Drinking habits. One ought never to speak of other people in a derogatory way — unless of course they were absolutely worthy of it, like Mrs. Harrower who gossiped, or Mr. Quincy who wouldn't let them walk through his woods to the pond. The family itself was never discussed with outsiders, nor, Lilian had noticed, with insiders either.

If you let a boy know you like him, Dolly Cushing went on, puffing on her cigarette, he'll think he can do whatever he wants. Her eyes narrowed as she related her experience with José Cutler.

Lilian remained mystified. As far as she could see Walter

Vail could do whatever he liked. If he liked it, she felt sure she would like it too.

The problem with you, said Dolly Cushing, is that you are too nice.

Yes, Lilian thought. She hoped no one would consider her to be something as bland as nice, and of course everyone did. She felt weak because of it. Thank goodness for Dolly who was telling her where she went wrong. She did not want to make a mistake with Walter Vail.

Can't wait to meet him, said Dolly whose interest in things quickly waned. Wait. Was he at the Spragues' the other day? With Madelaine! Good-looking, with a sort of tea stain on his face?

Lilian blushed to hear him described out in the world. Yes, she said. That's him. And feeling encouraged, Lilian told her about the rendezvous that evening.

Are you going to let him kiss you? Dolly asked. She wore satiny harem pants and a shirt with brocade trim on the sleeves. Lilian reflected how Jane Olney, dear stern Jane, would never have worn something so interesting, and felt glad to have a friend like Dolly Cushing who smoked cigarettes and asked about kissing. She supposed that a boy from New York, one so clearly at ease rubbing a girl's fingers as Walter Vail had done at the skating pond, would probably expect a kiss. It was just what Lilian needed to know. But her curiosity was unsatisfied as Dolly lost interest and began talking about the first time she had kissed Freddie Vernon at the country club dance. It was technically their first kiss, but the first long one came after on the shore at night where they watched the lighthouse blinking

1-4-3 which everyone knew meant I-love-you. Lilian could not imagine kissing Freddie Vernon. His poppy eyes and large nostrils made him look distinctly like a bulldog.

Lilian listened to Dolly, hoping to glean something instructive from her ramblings. She heard that a girl should always be interested in what a boy thought, that it was important to have the right sort of wrap, and that boys liked it if you hit them playfully on the arm. Dolly Cushing detailed her success with Freddie Vernon on these points. Dolly knew how to have fun, and if Lilian caught a little of her spirit she too might not take things so seriously. After leaving Dolly Cushing's house she walked home along a darkening Dartmouth Street and tried to digest this information. It seemed as if there were a web of interference circulating through her head, preventing her from having a clear thought.

3 · *The visitor from New York*

H E W A S a guest of the Fenwicks', staying with them through the holidays, and Madelaine Fenwick had been taking him around. Lilian first shook his hand at the Nobles' lunch the previous week and learned he was from New York.

He was there again at the Fenwicks' tea party a few days later, holding his back stiffly, still wearing the uniform. He had a straight nose, a finely defined mouth and a distracted air. Lilian placed him as one of those visitors who find life in Boston dull. As a Bostonian, Lilian could criticize Boston all she liked, but to an outsider she had the urge to defend it. He was not the sort of boy to be interested in Lilian Eliot, not that she would be drawn to him at all. Just the fact of his proximity to cold Madelaine Fenwick and his hovering over her by the tea tray was enough to put Lilian off. But he was in the armed forces, and it was hard not to be curious about someone ready to go off and fight.

When he said hello to Lilian he remembered her name, which threw her into confusion. She went to the opposite side of the room.

Some time later he reappeared. Running away from me? he said. He sat down on the needlepoint hassock almost at her feet.

I don't even know you.

We met last week, he said. Walter Vail.

Oh, yes.

You're not one of those Boston snobs, are you? Sniffy about people from New York?

She was taken aback. I don't know many people from New York, she said. Her Aunt Tizzy lived there, though she was from Boston, and there were Marian Lockwood's cousins from New York who used to visit at Easter, all smart clothes and ringlets, with a fondness for pickles.

I don't know many people from Boston, Walter Vail said.

Haven't you been meeting any this week?

I've been trying. He looked at her sideways.

She felt herself change a little under his gaze. I'm not one to tell you much, she said. I'm not one of those girls who goes to a dinner party for fourteen every night.

Is that what girls in Boston do?

Some of them.

And you're not a normal Boston girl?

I'm subnormal, she said.

Walter Vail expressed some interest in architecture about which Lilian knew a few things, having done some Saturdays with the Historical Society tours. He agreed with her that Hawthorne was preferable to Emerson, against the current fashion. As he spoke, there was something restless about him — Lilian imagined it had to do with his being in the forces — something urgent moving beneath the surface, hungry. Now and then his attention would be snatched up by someone passing, and he would glance up, startled, then return to her as if he hadn't known what had come over him, concentrating again, asking her questions.

He said, I played hockey with your brother yesterday.

Lilian found it odd he knew she and Arthur were brother and sister. Really?

Yes, an interesting fellow. Very amusing.

Not everyone thinks so, Lilian said.

He told me a little about you.

He did? Lilian found that odd too.

Walter Vail nodded. Lilian discovered she had no idea what he was like, the way she did with other boys.

Will you go overseas? she said.

The day after Christmas.

They both fell silent.

You want to go, Lilian said.

Got to see what it's all about over there, he said, sounding robust.

Don't your parents mind?

Al and Mimi? He shrugged.

Lilian had never heard of parents being called by their first names.

I suppose, but they're always away themselves. He hooked his hands around his knees, keeping his back straight. Steaming up from Brazil this week.

What does your father do?

Drinks mostly. Walter Vail laughed. He's a nice man — doing his best to make sure I have no inheritance.

Lilian stared at the talk of money. The Eliots were well off, not fancy, but well off. They were not rich like the Cunninghams or the Wiggins or the Cabots, but as Arthur liked to point out, their father did not exactly need to work. Nonetheless, he went to the law office six days a week, taking off two weeks' vacation a year, just as his father had. Lilian's grandfather's money came from banking and her grandmother, Henrietta Baker of the railroad Bakers, also had money. Lilian had never known exactly how much money there was. She knew only what her father had told her one Sunday afternoon, having summoned her to the library, and speaking of her future.

Walter Vail apparently did not have similar assurance.

. . . invested in the theatre, Walter Vail was saying. The fastest way to lose a fortune. But he met my mother — she was an actress then — backing a play she was in. The play went under, but he got Mimi out of it. He must wonder about his investment.

Lilian tried not to look shocked. She glanced down at Walter Vail's hands, clasped around his leg, and saw that they were normal-size hands and thought he was not so different. She felt reassured.

He said his parents were meeting him here, and Lilian asked him why not in New York.

My mother's cousin lives here.

In Boston? Who?

I don't think you'd know him, Walter Vail said. He lives on Lime Street when he's in town.

I know most of the names on the Hill, Lilian said, trying not to sound boastful.

Well, he's called Paul Harte. An artistic type.

Is he married? Lilian said.

Walter Vail hid a smile. Ah, no, he prefers being a bachelor, a different situation altogether.

Lilian nodded with a comprehending air, but had only a

vague notion of what he was getting at. Once again she came across the fact — the war made her think of it, too — that there were many different worlds far from the one she knew in Boston, though the way everyone around her behaved one would have thought Boston was the universe.

Later, sitting with a group among the cigar ashes and cold tea, Lilian watched Walter Vail across the room. He was laughing near the mantelpiece, his belt strapped across his chest, exhibiting a different, less intense personality from the one he'd shown her. Had she drawn special attention from him? It gave her a superior feeling to think so. Her thoughts were interrupted by Emmett Smith's whining at Elsie Sears who disagreed with him about the criteria needed to make the Social Register. It was the usual talk at tea, yet Lilian felt the world was not so usual. She supposed it was the war.

As the guests were leaving Walter Vail appeared in the coatroom and grabbed Lilian's wrist. I'd like to see you again, he said.

Was this how they did things in New York?

Well . . .

I mean it, he said, as if that were in question. There was a dark slant to his eyes, and she noticed a faint birthmark like a waterstain running down one cheek. He still held her wrist.

All right.

The Fenwicks used gas lamps in their hall, and in the rosy light Lilian glimpsed Madelaine Fenwick smiling, but with flat eyes, talking to a stooped fellow on his way out. She did not seem to care what her guest was doing with Lilian.

Walter Vail peered into the air. Then he thought of something. Do you skate?

Not well. Lilian thought of Madelaine Fenwick's skating trophies.

How about skating with us tomorrow? Bring along your brother. In the afternoon?

I will, said Lilian, and took back her wrist.

Good, said Walter Vail. He turned away abruptly, back straight, with the relieved air of someone having completed some distressing business.

I T WAS not unusual for Mr. and Mrs. Eliot to sit in the
same room for hours on end without exchanging a word.
That night Mr. Eliot sat at the living room desk, a cushion
pressed to his lower back, glancing at papers, with Mrs.
Eliot at her usual end of the Sheraton sofa, embroidering.
They'd eaten at seven and would be in bed by nine.

Mrs. Eliot stood. She wore a corset, but even without it
her carriage was erect. I'm going up, she said dimly, and
folded her cloth into the Chinese box and snapped shut the
lid.

Mr. Eliot grunted and bowed his white head.

Mrs. Eliot took the last sip from her sherry glass and
fingered the lace at her neck, considering something. The
ends of her mouth were upturned in a pleasant, blank
expression.

Above them past the bedrooms with canopy posts and
hallways with framed ancestral silhouettes, through the
low-eaved attic piled with striped hatboxes and slatted
trunks, out on the frozen slate roof in a gabled corner sat
Lilian. Her cheeks were the same as her mother's, smooth
and round, and her bottom lip protruded obstinately like
her father's, but the eyes were her own, liquid brown,
pooled and shiny.

The night was cold the way she liked it. Bits of light glinted in the sky. From where she sat she could see the dark mound of Beacon Hill, the candlelit windows here and there picking out a sliver of snow on the sill, and over the rooftops tilted stovepipes and dormers blacker than the sky. She was too low to see the harbor, but toward Cambridge she saw the Charles River with streetlamps making smudged reflections in the icy water.

It was the Christmas season, and all the going out put Lilian in a low mood. Of course, the talk always ended up being about the war and how wrong one felt breaking off ribbon candy and pouring brandy while the boys over there were freezing and nearly getting blown to bits every minute, and as her mother said, what would be the point sitting at home and being glum? Still, it disturbed. Tonight, after the Fenwicks', they'd thankfully dined at home and Lilian had got away as soon as possible. Her mother had tried to get her to eat more, thinking her too thin, and Lilian said in what she thought were perfectly polite tones that they could donate it to the effort which made Arthur laugh and Mr. Eliot turn his eagle profile to each of them to say that was enough. After dinner her nurse Hildy had been roaming around the second floor wanting to measure Lilian's new dress. Lilian had fled.

She wondered if the boys in France could see the same stars if they looked up, the same, that is, six hours before. Since the war, her own usual life had dwindled to a point — it was all so unimportant compared to what was going on over there. Her best friend Jane Olney's cousin Christopher had been with the Ambulance Corps for a year now, and wrote about having to drive thirty hours at a stretch and of seeing a boy with his face torn completely off. Whenever Lilian saw a boy in uniform she thought of how he might not come home. Charlie Sprague, whom she'd known since they'd ridden as children in the swan boats, had shipped over that fall, and Tommy Lattimore's brother enlisted despite his father's being against it. And there was that fellow from New York, Walter Vail . . .

She thought of Benjy Rogers and wondered if he were going over too. Not that she was thinking of him anymore, but he had said he was going last summer at the Promontory, though it had most likely been a boast to Nancy Cobb and, she had hoped at the time, to herself as well. But Nancy Cobb had had the advantage of having Benjy Rogers as her brother's house guest . . . The loss of his attentions may have bothered her then, but she was over it now — what a thing to be thinking about with the war on! She never even saw Benjy Rogers; he was from Philadelphia. Still, he was the last boy she'd thought of, with his socks rolled loose around his ankles and the way he colored quickly . . .

For a long time she had thought of George Snow who preferred tennis to girls and before that, Fellowes Moore, until he liked her back. Last summer she'd liked Jimmie Weld, but when the fall came he looked different back in Boston. There were the boys who came to call. Bayard Clark with his floating upper lip asked himself to dinner, and wheezing Reed Wheeler stopped in to relate his latest ailment. The Cunningham boys used to come with Marian Lockwood till she broke with Chip, stopping their bridge games. Emmett Smith brought everyone else's news, knowing all the families. Tommy Lattimore, with a long face like a wooden board, came whenever he could and colored pink when Lilian spoke directly to him. He was sweet, Tommy Lattimore, he read a great deal and during moments when he forgot himself would speak with eloquence on a subject he'd been studying, the Elgin Marbles or Etruscan tombs. Once Tommy Lattimore came and was surprised to see no other guests at the Eliots', he'd been told that Emmett Smith would be there. He had a tortured cup of tea with Lilian alone, and when he left she stood at the door taking in the fall air, watching him go down the brick sidewalk and turn the corner at Marlborough. Not once during his visit had he removed his hat.

As she went over the boys in her mind she tried to get used to the idea that she'd never find a boy right for her which would be all right; she wasn't planning on getting married. Aunt Tizzy hadn't, and she had an interesting life, only minding it sometimes. Still, being eighteen, Lilian wouldn't have minded having a beau.

She felt a rushing well up inside her: the outdoors made it happen. She breathed deeply to quiet it, trying to coax the feeling into a narrow stream which she might pour into a tiny cup where another might share it, but this was difficult to do. She felt as wide as the sky. And anyway was that how she was to pour herself out, in a little dribble when she felt herself to be a great wave? She held on to her laced boots, planted her chin on her knees and bore into the night. Sometimes she was amazed by the amount of feeling sloshing about inside her. If she let it out there would be a terrible flood, she thought — eddies in the parlor and waterfalls down the narrow stairs. And what would her mother make of that? It would not do.

Lilian considered the people around her in Boston, people she knew, people she didn't, walking up and down Beacon Street or Tremont Street or even their own Fairfield Street, and none of them revealed anything of what was going on inside. Either there was zero going on, which she did not believe, life was not like that, or they were carrying themselves with great dignity, being very brave, putting their feelings in one hidden place and the rest of themselves out in life. What amazed her was how seamlessly they managed it.

She had watched her mother's face below the seashell roll of hair while she straightened silverware in the sideboard, and could fathom none of the thoughts playing behind the shallow features. From a little window she'd spied on her father down on the back lawn, hands set in his pockets, on his way to discuss mulch with the gardener. But what was on his mind when he picked up a spindly branch and tossed it over the wall to Mrs. Youngman's and stood there and stared after it? Who could have said? And what of the milk delivery man who clattered white bottles in the wire holder? He had pocked cheeks, no eyelashes, and he hitched up his belt when he talked to Rosie.

There was life inside all of them and yet how secretly they kept it. She knew how difficult it was to do, and chances were if it was difficult, it was a good thing. She would learn to be the way they were and not show what was going on inside, not because it was the way everyone seemed, but because it was brave.

A dark lozenge with two ears appeared below her at the roof's edge. Arthur crawled up on all fours and sat next to his sister.

I was thinking about the boys, Lilian said, setting her jaw. She had a chin like a block, with a cleft in it, and dark eyes set off by flashing whites.

I'll be over there soon, said Arthur, his profile with an air of entitlement. As soon as he turned seventeen he was enlisting. Get some real material. Arthur had recently decided he was going to be a writer, like Oscar Wilde or Ambrose Bierce. Lilian could never have been an artist; her concerns were far too trivial. Arthur was the artistic one, the one who, when he gazed out at the night, saw colossal, universal things. While she didn't know any artists in person, she'd read about them and based her opinions on that.

What time is it? Arthur started up suddenly. He was like the fog, appearing out of nowhere, never able to stay still, and like the fog tending to obscure things.

Past nine.

Must go. He stretched out his long legs. While Arthur might say he was going for cards at the Cunninghams' or caroling at the Nobles', it was most likely a lie.

How's Amy Snow? said Lilian.

His sheepish smile was lit up by the streetlight. Wouldn't you like to know, he said and disappeared.

Her breath came out in a mist and she continued to sit, watching the night. She had the beginnings of ideas for happiness, but they were vague. Daydreaming was as close as she could get to them. She was beginning to see they were different from the ideas her parents had for her, her sense of happiness felt grand and sweeping, and theirs was small and tidy.

One day happiness would come to her. She did not think of it or expect it but sensed the faint ripening of it — a scene in the future, colored and polished and full of pleasant sounds. She would wait. It was the essence of life after all, and one needed patience. She was not as patient as she would have liked, but she was working on it.

THE SKY looked like snow and the air, drained of color, drew out the color in Lilian's cheeks.

Walter Vail was already out on the ice, a graceful figure taking long striding sweeps at the outer edge of the pond, his dark scarf loose on his army coat. Down at one end a game of curling was going on, and now and then a shout would rise from the ice. Madelaine Fenwick was nowhere in sight. Walter Vail spotted Lilian. She was wearing a wool coat with a center panel buttoned on either side and a beret with a checkered trim low to her eyes. He skated straight to her, cutting through the other skaters, the smile on his face so broad she glanced down.

You came, he cried, and struck an odd but appealing pose, between surprise and perplexity.

A few of us came over, Lilian said, and gestured toward Arthur and some of their friends. Walter Vail gave Arthur a hearty wave which Arthur returned with an ironic air, looking particularly sallow and dissipated this afternoon.

Lilian laced her skates without hurrying, finding a satisfaction for some reason in lingering. She put on her gloves and looked idly about for Arthur who had disappeared.

She stepped out onto the ice with Walter Vail who leaned toward her in an interested way.

I've been doing some investigating about you, he said. Lilian liked this, but wasn't sure what to make of it.

Dolly Cushing's brother Hugh skated by, a ball bobbing atop his hat, and Beany Wheeler passed with an extra look from behind his glasses. In the distance she saw Sis Cabot pushing her little sister on a chair, her figure bent and cranelike. The black branches stood out against the sky and Walter Vail's eyelashes stood out in his pale face, his breath trailing across in thin clouds. Lilian could not begin to fathom what was going on behind the mask face with the light birthmark running down it. Think of all the rooms he has seen, the views from high balconies, the dark doorways with candles shining inside . . . Lilian had only been to New York once, too young to remember more than an orange glow outside the windows at night and riding in a carriage with velvet. What she knew of it came from books or from Aunt Tizzy. Was it true that people traipsed about all night eating oysters and drinking champagne? Walter Vail's eyebrows rose. She was sounding quite the swell.

But what did she do in Boston? he wanted to know. She lunched with aunts, had tea with ladies. She'd graduated from the Peabody School for Girls — Lilian kept her high honors to herself — and was continuing with a course or two of study, at the moment with Mr. Holmes's lecture course on the History of Art. She went to concerts frequently, theatre rarely. One saw the same people in Boston. She viewed with some derision the Social Register. Boston was not like New York, filled with travelers. In Boston if a person went on a trip it would be to London, and he'd mention the crown jewels, the traffic noise in Piccadilly, and how foggy it had been. She recalled one Christmas on Beacon Street when Uncle Nat — that was her father's brother — had turned his blank face to ask Aunt Tizzy what she wanted to travel for. Aunt Tizzy's painted eyes rolled ceilingward. You were born in Boston, Uncle Nat persisted, why go anywhere else? To get away from people like you, Aunt Tizzy said, which made Lilian's father laugh, but he was the only one.

Walter Vail listened to her, amused, as if he were adding up all the things which went into her and laying them out for contemplation.

Lilian was not apologizing for Boston, she said, tucking her chin into her collar, but she could see how someone could find it dull.

His look had some discomfort which she liked him for. He said he wasn't finding it dull in the least.

She mentioned her hands were getting cold, meaning they should go in, and before she knew it Walter Vail had stopped her on the ice and taken one glove in his bare hands to rub at her fingers in a smooth, natural way. It was clear this was not out of the ordinary for him to be warming a girl's hand. Her whole body had a strange relaxed feeling.

Over Walter Vail's shoulder she saw Arthur down at the other end of the pond near the curling players. He was up on the bank, talking to some young people she'd never seen before. One girl was dressed in a long cape, and the other boys wore hats set at angles. All were smoking. Around them was an air of raciness, and decay.

WHO WERE your friends? Lilian asked Arthur. They were on their way to Fairfield Street where they'd asked Walter Vail for tea.

Arthur had learned from his father to ignore questions of no interest to him and talked about the curling game. Did she know that the Finch brothers were national champions?

Of curling? Lilian said, kicking open the heavy door.

The house on Fairfield Street had two halls, one a narrow entryway where light from a lead-starred window made patterns on the floor, then the wider proper hallway with a standing grandfather clock and green Chinese urns standing empty. White shelves in the corner displayed china, a plate and two vases on one shelf, a pair of parrots flanking a tureen on the next, china baskets and so on. Plates were decorated with eagles, arrows crossed beneath their claws, or trimmed with borders of blue and gold. The Canton china, blue and white pagodas and bridges, was in the dining room and got used. On a narrow table with wood inlays, beneath a distorting mirror, was a shallow china dish with straight sides where the mail was placed twice a day.

The library had the smell of smoky tea. There were chairs with leather seats and backs attached to wooden arms and legs by brass studs. A low sofa faced the fireplace, a potted palm leaned toward a corner window.

The living room did not look so different though it was larger, with bookshelves lining the walls and two blue Sheraton sofas facing each other. There was a standing lamp with a ruffled trim, Persian rugs on the floor, and if it were summer a side table holding a glass bowl of rhododendrons from the bush outside. On the desk near the green blotter with leather sides, the leather-handled letter opener and the decorative cut glass inkwells were pieces of driftwood dotted with carved sea birds in different poses. Some were simply standing, others had wings spread, posed to take flight.

It was a Saturday and Mr. and Mrs. Eliot were dining out, so Rosie was not in the kitchen slapping at a roast. The days were still getting shorter and a weak yellow light could be glimpsed out the windows. It was Hildy's day off and the house seemed especially quiet. While Lilian made the tea, sounds echoing in the high-ceilinged room, Arthur and Walter Vail loitered in the hall, glancing through doorways to the dining room, the living room. Walter Vail held his head back and picked out the Copley portrait above the mantelpiece and Arthur commended him, hands in pockets, eyes low-lidded, expressing little in his monotone, on having selected the most precious painting in the room.

They lit a fire in the library and Lilian brought the tea tray out from the gloom of the pantry. Arthur smoked a cigarette near an open window with the furtiveness of one not allowed tobacco. The cold air drew the smoke out in a graceful line.

It was pleasant to have Walter Vail there. His interest in

Lilian made for an extra glow in the room as they chatted by the fire. She held herself upright, her brown eyes, intent, glanced out from a level brow. At the moment, he fancied her more than she did him. She wasn't sure what she thought of him, liking his attention, feeling he was different. The boys she knew would find nothing unusual in her being a girl from Boston. It made her feel different too.

D'you know anyone over there? Lilian said.

Why sure, a few.

Forrey Cooper, from where we go in Maine, just joined the navy, Lilian said. He's only sixteen.

He is not sixteen, said Arthur. More like eighteen. Arthur was usually right about these things.

Well it's young either way, she said. How old are you?

Walter Vail braced himself in an odd way against the sofa arm, uncomfortable to be answering questions about himself. Twenty, he said. For an instant Lilian wondered if he were lying.

She handed him a second cup of tea and he met her gaze with a penetrating stare, shocking her. She had the feeling he was testing her with rules from a world she didn't know. She unbent herself to put another log on the fire. Sitting back down, having composed herself, she watched him talk, not having the least idea what he was saying.

They heard some stomping at the door. Mr. Eliot came in first, the coat closet being just outside the library, and appeared to detect Arthur's smoke, his face sharp and disapproving, the round reflection of his glasses hiding the expression in his eye. They'd been visiting old Uncle Bill in Brookline.

Who have we here? Mr. Eliot said, and Walter Vail leapt across the room to shake hands. Mr. Eliot, not accustomed to sudden physical contact, recoiled a little. Mrs. Eliot emerged from the murky hall, pulling vaguely at her gloves. Lilian introduced her guest.

Oh yes, said Mrs Eliot. Diana told me they had you. She kept her face half-turned as if waiting to decide what she made of this person. With a mixture of sincerity and shyness, Walter Vail told them how greatly he admired the house and to Mrs. Eliot how beautifully he thought she'd arranged it. She wore a dazed expression. Arthur, leaning back on the arm of a chair, smirked. Lilian gave him a cross look.

Won't you sit down? Walter Vail said. The Eliots had yet to be invited by a guest to sit in their own house.

Of course, said Mrs. Eliot, and she removed her hat, arms reaching deftly, without tipping her head one degree.

Mr. Eliot strode further into the room and stood stiff-kneed by the tea tray. He lit a cigar and asked Walter Vail about his army training. Camp had not been so interesting, Walter Vail replied, an opinion Mr. Eliot did not seem to appreciate. He paused, too, when he heard Walter Vail utter the distasteful phrase 'the excitement overseas.'

Isn't your mother the actress? said Mrs. Eliot, surprised she'd remembered.

Used to be.

I suppose one must be a sort of exhibitionist to be an actress, Mrs. Eliot said.

On the mantel a clock chimed and was echoed more faintly by the standing clock in the hall. Oh my God, said

Walter Vail, using an expression Mrs. Eliot often checked in Arthur. He stood up. I didn't realize the time. The Fenwicks will be expecting me.

In the outer hall with the door opened Lilian said goodnight. Walter Vail had a peculiar expression, a cross between pain and curiosity. He cupped Lilian's round cheek with his hand and, as he stepped back, let his fingers run along her jaw.

Lilian told her mother she'd asked him for dinner on Monday night.

Shouldn't we have Madelaine? Mrs. Eliot said.

I don't see why, Lilian said. She wasn't skating.

All that evening Lilian found she could gaze for long periods of time at nothing in particular and be perfectly content.

L ILIAN SAT with a book in the cheery light of the
living room, staring at the same paragraph over and
over again, feeling ill, wishing she'd never met Walter Vail,
wishing her father had let him come to dine, and wishing
she'd never arranged for him to be knocking on her french
doors at any moment. The Christmas tree was up in the
corner, lit with candles, and the room had a milky glow.
Outside the night was clear, and through the black windows of the ominous doors she could see clumps of snow in
ghostly shapes in the garden.

Finally the tap came, it was rather soft.

Lilian sprang up. She had worn an old dress, a favorite
green one with white bands, to feel that it was herself he
was seeing and not something wrapped in pretty new
things, and had not brushed her hair, wanting to appear
natural. She wore her collars loose, never below the collarbone, and had good straight shoulders. The only real jew-
elry she had was a locket with a picture of her parents on
one side and Hildy on the other which tonight she wore
close to the skin.

She went to the door, feeling her throat thickening, and
the cold came in when she opened it. Walter Vail had a

look of wonder as if he were bringing her the happiest news
and immediately she was glad he'd come.

We have to stay quiet, she said.

Did you have a nice dinner without me? Walter Vail
whispered.

Having to whisper, they stayed close. Lilian took him on
a tour of the room, ignoring that he'd been there before
with Arthur. They gave rapt attention to each inconsequential thing, analyzing Uncle Nat's shadow boxes and
giving much consideration to the titles of the burning ship
prints. Walter Vail listened, absorbed, while Lilian pointed
out who was who in the framed photographs on the tables
and told where the carved birds had come from. He stood
near as they examined the ostrich egg set on a little ring
stand which Aunt Tizzy had brought back from Africa.
Lilian turned her face — his was very close to hers, smiling.

Shall we sit down? she said. It occurred to her she was
not showing an interest in what he was thinking.

They sat near the fire. Their talk was of little consequence to anyone but themselves, idle and light, the sort
found when two people find delight in each other's company. Walter Vail spoke about becoming an architect, but
wondered if he had the discipline for it. Lilian told him that
of course he did. He was also concerned with the financial
insecurity of the profession. Lilian wondered again if it was
New York — bringing up money and speaking of it in the
open. Lilian could not remember the subject's being discussed at their dinner table except by Arthur, who wondered aloud how much the Morses had spent on their
dancing party or why Mr. Cunningham traveled second

class when he could have bought the whole train. Then Arthur would be silenced by his father and the discussion would go no further.

It seemed therefore to Lilian that Walter Vail was confiding in her. At one moment she caught herself looking at his mouth as though hypnotized. She snapped out of it. She had been kissed by a boy before, but not by one like Walter Vail.

It was after midnight when Walter Vail snuck out the front door. They made plans to have lunch the next day, somewhere in town. He kissed her on the cheek, and it seemed to linger there after he'd gone.

Lilian spent the following morning in a dreamy haze. Then at twelve o'clock, the time appointed for their meeting, Walter Vail did not show.

At three o'clock Lilian received a note with the afternoon mail.

> So sorry to have missed lunch. The parents arrived. We're to spend a few days on the North Shore. I'll see you when I get back.
>
> Your accomplice,
Walter Vail

And in a weak pencil underneath, as an afterthought, *Sorry*.

Lilian felt the lovely construction which had gone up around her splinter and fall to the ground. She went purposefully up to her room to avoid meeting anyone and once there stood at her bureau looking at the little boxes on it, the silver one with her initials, the pillbox with the black cat on it. She moved the white-bristled hairbrush to a different place on the linen runner, she lifted the tortoiseshell top of her hairpin box. She could feel tears welling behind her eyes and was ashamed. Why had he taken so long to write? Perhaps his parents had surprised him. Whatever had happened, it was clear that this had not mattered so much to him as to her. So, she would not let it matter so much either.

In the following days she was in a foul mood. She reported to Dolly Cushing the latest events, and Dolly said that now was the time to remain aloof, if he were interested he would have to do the work. Since this tactic ran counter to Lilian's natural feelings, she felt sure that it must be correct.

THE CUNNINGHAMS gave only one party a year, not wanting to be ostentatious, an eggnog party the Friday before Christmas. Lilian did not want to go, feeling too listless to socialize, but her parents would not hear of leaving her behind. Whole families attended the Cunninghams' Christmas party. Living nearby, the four Eliots walked there, Arthur not wearing an overcoat as if it were a spring night.

Marian Lockwood was the first person Lilian ran into when she stepped inside the door. At first she was surprised to see her there, Marian had broken off with Chip Cunningham that fall. Everyone had assumed there would be an engagement in the summer — though Aunt Tizzy said she knew they wouldn't, obviously lacking the spark — but Marian had decided against it. Lilian had known Marian since infancy, a plump-armed, exuberant girl who was cozy with you as long as she got what she wanted, which she usually did. The oldest of five girls, Marian Lockwood was accustomed to telling people what to do. Clearly, she had wanted to come to the Christmas party and had simply told Chip Cunningham, a weak fellow with an indecisive face, who was powerless to say no.

Familiar with the Cunningham house, Marian Lockwood was right at home. What a pretty color, Marian said about Lilian's dress. The Lockwood girls did their clothes buying in New York under their cousins' guidance and took great interest in fashion. Tell me where you found it.

Irene Minter was there. Lilian was glad to see her. Irene Minter seemed to exist in another world, pale, black-eyed, lifted apart by an inner distraction, troubled by private things. Her hair was the color of pale wheat. Irene was always asking unanswerable questions, something which annoyed people but which Lilian liked, intrigued more by her manner than by the odd things she came up with. Irene had artistic talents, something Lilian admired, and the Cunninghams had a little watercolor she'd done of a boat which they'd bought at a benefit art show. Irene was showing the little painting with great embarrassment to her escort who looked as if he'd stepped out of an Arrow Shirt advertisement.

Why, you look wonderful, Irene Minter said, her black eyes wondrous. Is it love? She introduced Lilian to her friend, a fellow previously unknown to her. Irene Minter tended to go around with handsome men, sleepy-eyed and vague, who seemed hardly to notice her.

Dolly Cushing was there, hair glinting, dressed in something with rows of scallops and showing off a new pair of strap shoes. Striking just the wrong note, Dolly winked hello. Lilian's mood was low. Mr. Cunningham called her Ellen, and Mrs. Cunningham extended an invitation to her daughter Elizabeth's birthday the next month. Elizabeth Cunningham was younger than Lilian, but their families being friends, she'd have to go. Elizabeth, frightened and graceless, did not have many friends of her own.

After a dinner of glazed ham and creamed onions eaten on plates set on knees, the adults with younger children drifted home while the others went into the smaller sitting rooms to drink. This left the young people to their own amusements.

Dolly Cushing and Harry Cunningham, the more jovial brother, organized a game which everyone just had to play. They shouted and pointed to people to arrange themselves in a correct way. Lilian saw Madelaine Fenwick in a satin-trimmed dress sitting apart with a superior air. Lilian skulked to the back of the room to brood, finding a chair against the wall near a heavy curtain. Arthur who hated parlor games joined her, sensing her mood, silent, thrusting out the Eliot chin as he sat down. Irene Minter took a chair nearby and Arthur's face took on a cloudy look, following the movements of her hands as she traced her odd notions in the air. Irene Minter appears haunted tonight, Lilian thought. But then, nothing seemed right. Irene's escort stared with slack mouth at the proceedings.

Freddie Vernon was the head of one team. His high collar appeared to be choking him, that or it was simply the effect of his protruding eyes. Chip Cunningham stood off to the side, tortured by Marian Lockwood's thumb-wrestling with Dickie Wiggin, a shy dapper fellow who couldn't believe his luck. Lilian had a momentary start when out of the corner of her eye she caught sight of a belted army jacket, but it was only Tommy Lattimore's brother who was also shipping out after Christmas. Scattered about on the stiff sofas and old armchairs, the young people sat with upraised eyes as one person after another stood before them making mysterious gestures, pointing at parts of their body, holding up fingers, drawing pictures in the air and contorting themselves on the floor. Amidst the shouting Lilian noticed one quiet face: Tommy Lattimore's doleful gaze, directed at her.

All evening she had been unable for a moment to stop thinking of Walter Vail and of when he would be returning from the North Shore.

Just then timid Elizabeth Cunningham, head drooped forward, led a new arrival into the room. Chip, she said softly, and sad Chip looked wanly over. Harry, she said, and when Harry looked, the group turned. Dolly let out a hoot and looked immediately toward Lilian who shrank back into the curtain. It was Walter Vail.

Sorry — I — I'm late, he said with a twisted face full of feeling. We only just returned . . . But his explanation was drowned out; no one cared, he was here now. Harry Cunningham slapped his back and drew him into the circle of chairs. Lilian, rooted to her seat, watched as Walter Vail feigned ignorance then caught on with alarming ease. Lilian felt herself shrivel. Seeing him in the flesh wiped out some of the more dazzling qualities she remembered. He's not as handsome as I'd thought, she reflected. In fact, he's hardly remarkable at all. That her whole body felt charged with a current upon his arrival she did not consider. He leaned forward with the group, engrossed, with no intention whatsoever of meeting her eye.

Finally, the game broke up and the guests began to leave. After chatting with Madelaine Fenwick, Walter Vail crossed the room to where a stony-faced Lilian Eliot sat inspecting the folds in her lap.

Hello there, he said.

Lilian looked up and involuntarily smiled. You're back, she said.

You weren't playing, he said.

She shrugged, unable to stop smiling.

I'm sorry about last week, he said.

Lilian didn't say anything, wanting him to stay sorry.

Something came up, he said.

Oh? she said, and found she could stop smiling.

Walter Vail did not seem especially concerned. It reminded Lilian of Arthur who didn't care if anyone believed him or not. They were similar too in that one could not rely on Arthur either, not for practical things. For some reason Lilian had always believed that Arthur's intentions were good, perhaps even better than most people's. Look at how he was always pointing out unfairness. Why didn't Rosie get more than one day off a week? Why did Mrs. Eliot ask Mrs. Amory over if she didn't like her? True, he caused trouble, but he didn't hide it, he admitted it. Something had to be said for that. There was Arthur now near the ivy-trimmed entryway, his thin neck straining forward, tilting his head to catch each breathy word Irene Minter uttered, as if it were too distracting to look at her directly. To Lilian, Arthur had a saintly quality mixed in with his devilish ways.

And here, standing before her, a number of the qualities belonging to Arthur seemed to appear in Walter Vail. In that light, she felt she understood Walter Vail better — he was like Arthur who meant well even though it didn't always turn out that way. She so much did not want to be one of those girls who didn't understand a boy.

Are you angry with me? Walter Vail said. He sat down in Arthur's seat. He took her arm.

No, she said, and her arm turned into something else with his hand on it, something otherworldly, while the rest of her remained as before. She did not look at him, hoping to stay aloof as Dolly Cushing had advised. She could feel him checking her expression, expecting her anger. But what claim did she have on him? She was not about to let him know he mattered in the least. And if she was mad? She'd never expressed anything of the sort, except to her family, and even if she had felt confident to do so, which she didn't, she would not have chosen the Cunninghams' Christmas party as the backdrop.

Walter Vail explained how they'd gone to Prides Crossing to visit the bachelor uncle who had a small house by the sea in addition to the house around the corner on Lime Street where the Vails were staying now. Lilian was glad to hear he was no longer at the Fenwicks'. He said his mother loved to visit the North Shore even in winter, and so they'd left straight from the dock when their ship landed. Walter Vail had spent the summer there the previous year and was fond of his uncle.

There were lots of people we had to visit, he said. I didn't know we'd stay so long. He checked Lilian's expression again, but she was doing her best to reveal nothing. Now that we're staying so close we can see each other without my having to sneak in the garden door, he said. Though I wouldn't mind.

Lilian smiled.

I am sorry, he said in a softer tone.

Lilian nodded.

I thought you'd understand, he said.

Against all her instincts, Lilian shrugged. It was only lunch, she said offhandedly.

Walter Vail looked down, frowning with mild perplexity. The stain on his cheek appeared darker. Oh, he said, and with a shock Lilian realized that he was not looking down in embarrassment but was checking his buttoned pockets to locate his folded cap. Was that all? Would he try so little?

Now he was standing up. Now he glanced at her, disappointed, desperate to be gone. Oh, what would Dolly say to this? Let him go? Yes, let him go and he'd think it over, he'd realize she was not a girl to be pushed around, that she was a spirited girl, one to contend with, and then he'd be back.

But would he? Lilian's mind was racing. It wasn't as if he were a regular boy from Boston who lived a few streets away on Mount Vernon or Willow, or even that he was returning to New York the day after tomorrow, even New York was not so far away but he was going much farther. He was going overseas, and he might never come back.

He was heading for the door.

Lilian watched him.

He was looking about for one of the Cunninghams in order to say good-bye.

Wait, Lilian said. I'll come out with you.

9 · *The beautiful hour*

WHEN THEY stepped out of the Cunninghams' doorway into a small courtyard their faces were grazed
by the feathery touch of snowflakes. The street was covered
with a white dusting, and the other guests exclaimed how
lovely it looked.

Walter Vail proposed a walk. It was a still night and the
black air streamed with drifting down.

They set out toward the Common where the lights were
most bright and strolled through the luminous air along
the paths marked with looping chains. Their arms brushed
each other and they stayed close and it continued to happen. When they crossed the street back toward the Hill,
Walter Vail took her arm, and on the other side — there
were hardly any cars on the roads — he kept hold of it. He
told her about his time in Prides Crossing. They had gone
to a dinner — she should have seen — clam chowder then
chicken, cauliflower and potatoes — everything white! —
even dessert, something called Floating Island — and Lilian was grateful for his saying, You wouldn't have believed
it, thinking her like him, since she would have found nothing at all unusual in such a meal.

They navigated a steep hill. His arm went around her,
palm scooping her elbow, holding tight.

{ 42 }

She had never been gripped by a boy the way Walter Vail was gripping her. He steered her along the sidewalks, a winter night where no one saw, and he couldn't have done it if she hadn't let him, but she did. She felt like someone else. I feel it because of him, she thought. The person he sees is quite different from the one I feel myself to be — it's a better person Walter Vail sees. She preferred that person.

She felt like someone she might have read about in a book or seen in a play, only she wasn't pretending or acting out a part — she had the feeling to go with it, a feeling everywhere in her, poured into her body like liquid brass into a mold. It pooled through her, taking her over. She felt lifted a few inches from the ground, arms weightless, legs strong, her hips aware of the loose slip against them, the weight of her dress on the slip, and on top of it all her bulky coat. They were on Pinckney Street and the lanterns picked out snow falling, the bricks already covered with a flour dusting and here and there a few footprints showing. They walked up tilted sidewalks and followed curving streets.

It was she who stopped. She planted herself in front of him thinking how he would not be here long, maybe never here again, and as he looked at her she had time to wonder if he knew what she meant, but there was no worry in her wonder, worry had been left back in the yellow-lit room with the potted poinsettias where the cups had white coins of eggnog left, and the embers were red in the fireplace and the talk of nothing close to anyone's heart, she thought, at least not like here where worry left off. Where she was now with Walter Vail the world was a deserted stage set, the sounds padded off, muffled behind the beaded curtain of snow, the slender houses with their narrow fronts and granite steps and paper layer of down, a lantern tied with ivy near the door, a wreath in shadow, the glint of a knocker and down the street the dark shape of a person walking a dog. She stopped. Her hand rested on an iron gate post and she brushed off a little peak of snow coyly and looked him in the eye. She was weightless and strangely bold. It was a wonderful thing to look into a boy's eye and not be ashamed. Walter Vail's eyes, dark in the center, were like another land and she found gazing into that land to be the most natural thing in the world. It was a landscape she could have flown over, taking in the different casts of light: clear sky here, then dark clouds there, off in the distance a still field, and closer by, trees blowing on a round hill. It was dusk, evening, the beautiful hour. Looking into his eyes, she believed in treasure. She could have gazed forever, still young enough to think of forever as a possible length of time.

He put his hands on her shoulders, brushing off snow, and her head leaned back when his face came close. She closed her eyes, shy to be this near, and was stunned with what happened inside her. There was a deep pounding and she swooned. Her eyes parted slightly to see his cheek magnified this near, and there was his nose brushing hers. She'd never imagined such an altering. It was as if she'd become velvet blackness. Her head was no longer of any consequence, and her body felt so many new things. After a moment she gasped for air.

I couldn't help — Walter Vail began.

Oh, no, Lilian said, falling toward him.

He kissed her again and the miraculous disturbance continued.

It was some time later that, beaded with snow, she lifted a sleepy, glistening face to Walter Vail, and bid him goodnight at the Fairfield Street door. It is finally happening to me, she thought.

THE NEXT DAY Walter Vail returned to Fairfield Street, coming out of a bright day with snow shining on the roofs and eaves dripping. He and Lilian slipped into the dark library. No fire had been set, but it was the most private room in the house. Mrs. Eliot was out for the morning.

Lilian closed the door behind her and waited for Walter Vail to surround her with his arms, but he had become shy. He gravitated toward a far wall and peered with great earnestness at a framed eighteenth-century map of Cape Cod with a large starry compass in one corner. He asked her about it. Lilian, not understanding his behavior, smiled as she answered him, trying to encourage him, but grew less at ease. He'd been to Cape Cod one summer with the Fenwicks, he said in an unnaturally loud voice, but too long ago to remember. Did she go there? Did she like it? Yes, Lilian said, she'd always liked the sea, though Maine was her favorite . . . Her voice had a hollow timber to it, her thoughts elsewhere. It occurred to her that Walter Vail had not told her of his feelings. Perhaps she had misunderstood.

The conversation faltered.

In the dead silence Walter Vail said, I can't have dinner with you tonight. He picked up a brass owl and pulled back its hinged head.

It was to be their last night. Oh? Lilian smiled weakly.

There's someone I have to see, he said, thoroughly engrossed with inspecting the figurine. Is this for cigarettes? he said.

Lilian didn't answer, suddenly so far from him. Your parents? she said, knowing he would have said if it was.

No. He put the owl down. His hands went into his pockets. He sighed. It's someone I had been seeing a while ago, but . . . He gestured in an odd way, arms akimbo, glancing with annoyance at Lilian as if she were to blame for putting him through this discomfort. I saw her in Prides Crossing last week. His head hung off a guilty neck.

You did? Blood drained from Lilian's face, from her heart. Everything stopped.

She's not someone who . . . I mean, I've known her a long time . . . before I met you . . .

Lilian was speechless. She did not want to hear another word. She wanted to hear every detail.

I hadn't seen her for a while, Walter Vail added lamely. Then he shut up.

Lilian glanced at the window where the part in the dark curtains revealed a blinding white day outside. Finally she spoke. Do I know her? Her voice had thinned to a thread.

I don't think so. Walter Vail cast his gaze downward, frowning arduously.

Well, who is it? Lilian felt absolutely hard.

She's just . . . It's Nita Russell. Walter Vail glanced at

Lilian, pleading, checking how this information affected her. He immediately looked away.

Lilian sat down on the sofa. I know her, she said, staying very still. I thought she was engaged to one of the Reeds. Her voice was flat, absent of interest.

Well she was, Walter Vail began. It's, well, it's turned into a big mess.

Lilian stared at the curved handle on the butler's table, following its shape around and around. So are *you* going to marry her? she said, surprised at her boldness.

God, no, Walter Vail burst out. His personality seemed to return, and he nearly laughed.

Lilian looked up.

I just have to talk with her, Walter Vail said, shrinking in her gaze.

Lilian nodded. Nita Russell, she said. I always thought she was quite something.

She's sort of crazy, Walter Vail said. High-strung.

While it had occurred to Lilian that Walter Vail had known other girls, she'd not thought of them as actually existing. Of course they did. So, the girls he liked were high-strung, with swelling chests and clouds of yellow hair like Nita Russell's.

The room was silent. The clock ticked. Lilian sat up a little and tried to compose herself.

I just feel sorry for her, Walter Vail said, and cleared his throat.

The Nita Russell Lilian knew was a striking girl who always appeared poised and in some private way intrigued with herself. She was not someone to feel sorry for in the least. Lilian's lower lip protruded, brooding.

She broke her engagement on my account, he said. His hands flew into the air. I have to have dinner with her. His exasperation suddenly seemed genuine.

Perhaps he really was in a bind. Lilian had heard of Nita Russell's getting into other intrigues.

I should think so, Lilian said.

I'd much rather be with you, Walter Vail said under his breath, then seeing the effect it had, added, I really would.

It seemed to Lilian he did mean it. She felt some of the old power returning. He must have seen it in her expression for he dared approach her. He sat down beside her.

She did not pull away. She noticed how his shoulders filled out the rough wool of his jacket. She touched his arm. He was close to her again, and when she saw his face this near the Walter Vail of the night before reappeared: she knew the eyes, this near. His attention bore down sweetly on her. He took her hand. She found it difficult to think straight when he took her hand, but it seemed to ground her. In fact, it was the most certain thing of all, his warm hand.

You're some girl, he said.

No I'm not, she said. I'm like all the other girls, except Nita Russell. I'm not like her.

No, Walter Vail said, and he put his arm around her small-boned shoulders. The quiet in the room changed from a stiff and worried one. Thank goodness you're not.

DOLLY CUSHING could hardly wait to give Lilian her impressions of Walter Vail and to find out where they had gone off to. Dolly stopped over after lunch, carrying shopping bags, and showed Lilian the presents she'd bought.

But he is terribly charming, she said. If I didn't have Freddie . . . Dolly rolled her shoulders in a provocative way. I was watching him at the Cunninghams'. He didn't take his eyes off you.

Lilian winced, wishing she'd kept the whole business to herself.

Dolly regarded her friend with a solemn face. Marry him, she said.

Lilian laughed, and turned her face to hide the blush. I've known him for a week, she said. It was the silliest idea she'd ever heard. Inside, however, something different was going on, the passing thought met with a strange note of reality, as if the idea of marrying Walter Vail had already taken up residence and was surprising her there, already in the room, settled in an armchair. Someone who knew Lilian better like Jane Olney, still down in Florida through January, might have suspected this deeper feeling, but

Dolly Cushing had only a slight acquaintance with deeper feeling and had little notion of what her friend was going through.

Lilian related the facts concerning Nita Russell, treating her interference as something inconsequential, but Dolly immediately took it up as an intrigue.

This, she said, is dangerous. You must come to an agreement with him. And she proceeded to enumerate the various ways to do this. As she talked her voice took on a distant buzz, like flies on a summer day, leaving Lilian's mind free to wander. She was recalling her kiss with Walter Vail. She knew better than to mention this to Dolly. She thought of the warm fingers of Walter Vail's hand, she could feel them on her cheek, and as long as she thought of these things, Nita Russell was not a thought at all. Besides, she was seeing Walter Vail tonight! They'd arranged to meet after his dinner with Nita Russell. Why would he arrange a meeting if he weren't interested?

Dolly left in a bustle of boxes and tissue paper and Lilian sank back into her reverie. But this time Nita Russell appeared. Lilian found herself picturing Walter Vail kissing the tall girl. Lilian was sure they had! His arm was curved around her back; she bent against it. Lilian watched in horror as the hand which moments before had been so soothing on her cheek became an image of torture as she watched it unbuttoning the pearl buttons of Nita Russell's blouse and slipping inside.

SHE WAS so distracted she would have preferred to forgo dinner altogether that night, but Aunt Tizzy had arrived for her Christmas visit, bringing with her a whiff of the outer world, and Lilian liked to hear what she had to say. If it weren't for Aunt Tizzy, she would never know there were interesting aspects to the Eliot family, such as their mother's having always gone barefoot in spring or Mr. Eliot being kept overnight in jail for being an unruly youth, that is, for drinking. When Lilian asked her father what life had been like before she was born, he told her matter-of-factly that it was quite the same as it was now.

With her head full of Walter Vail and encouraged by Aunt Tizzy's presence, by her sparkling bracelets and thin crimson lips, by her hair afrizz around her pale face, Lilian asked her father how he and Mrs. Eliot had met. She'd heard the story before, but it hadn't been for some time — it had to do with a meeting involving a picnic and some lost gloves. Lilian was interested in meetings.

Mr. Eliot, who had married relatively late in life, regarded his daughter as if she were an interrogator trying to get him to speak. He wasn't going to be tricked. You ask your mother about that, he said.

Mrs. Eliot sat at the far end of the table, blinking with contentment, her nose in a wineglass.

What about your mother and father? Lilian asked. Mr. Eliot's parents had died within a month of each other during a flu epidemic in 1882. Mr. Eliot had been twenty. Aunt Tizzy, being ten years younger — their brother Uncle Nat was in the middle — had gone to live with cousins in Dover.

They knew each other in Boston, Mr. Eliot said, indicating this was the entire story. Above the highboy was an oval painting in a gold frame of a small boy in ringlets and a ruffled dress. My Father When He Was a Little Girl, Mr. Eliot called it.

They met in a war relief office, said Aunt Tizzy. That's how Uncle Charlie told it. Mother was doing nursing work and Father had been wounded . . .

Father was never enlisted, said Mr. Eliot.

He most certainly was, said Aunt Tizzy. I have his cap.

Just because a man has a cap doesn't mean he was a Union soldier.

Not this again, said Arthur.

Mr. Eliot regarded his son with collapsed lids. You watch your impertinence, he said.

With interest, said Arthur.

Someday that attitude will get you in trouble.

Let's hope, said Arthur.

Lilian had seen pictures of all the dead grandparents in the boxes in the attic: studio envelopes with flared script and embossed violets, people sitting on porches cascading with saucer-shaped leaves, women holding babies, men with pipes, a dog in midair jumping at someone's hand. Who were they all? Lilian was curious about what they thought and what they said and how they met and how the world had seemed to them then. She was especially interested in Mrs. Eliot's mother, Lilian Baker, for whom she'd been named. She'd died in childbirth, leaving Mrs. Eliot to be raised by a stepmother and a resentful father. According to Mrs. Eliot, her father never forgave her. Lilian Baker was half-French and in one picture she wore a black dress with satin ribbons undulating over it. There was a blur across her eyes.

Soon they were talking about the war.

Arthur cleared his throat. I was wondering —

Mr. Eliot interrupted him. A man came into my office today. 'I was wondering,' he said, and proceeded to chatter on about some nonsense. 'Are you asking me a question?' I said. He looked at me as if I were mad. What is this 'I was wondering' business? It's as bad as 'I don't know but.'

Mr. Eliot did not practice in the courtroom but treated his dining room as one.

Should I listen to someone who begins his sentence with 'I was wondering' or 'I don't know but'? Certainly not.

Mrs. Eliot, smiling pleasantly, waved her hand in front of her face the way one waves away smoke.

I was wondering, Arthur repeated, if I might be excused.

Mr. Eliot stared at him stonily.

May I please be excused? said Arthur.

To what purpose?

Harry Cunningham's having cards.

Alice wouldn't like that, said Mrs. Eliot, shaking her head vaguely.

Do Alice good, said Aunt Tizzy. A little life in the house.

Arthur let out a whine of exasperation.

Mr. Eliot slipped a watch out of his pocket. Go on, he said, not pleased.

Arthur bolted out through the swinging pantry door back into the kitchen to thank Rosie for the roast and the cake. Casey the butler and Hildy with her starched front would be sitting down to their dinner with Rosie at the enamel table, and Mary at the sink would have started on the dishes. Above them, up the narrow back stairs, were their rooms jumbled together — the halls rugless, a lamp in each room — a place Lilian and Arthur used to spend a lot of time, lying on Hildy's chenille spread, cranking her music box, asking if she'd ever get married. Hildy, who'd raised Lilian and Arthur and now looked after Mrs. Eliot's clothes as well, said she was far too old for that business. She was from Norway, with a proud manner and wide arms which in their vigilance had sometimes threatened to smother the little Eliots. Lilian had been drawn to the warmth of the kitchen where she watched Mary ironing with a blue-veined arm or Casey dismantle the epergne for polishing. Then as she got older she went there less frequently and knew little about Mary's sailor beau or about the new girl Shirley who came in for the linens. Now when she saw the back rooms it was to thank Rosie for dinner, or for lemonade on a hot summer afternoon, or for Rosie's cocoa in the winter, but even then the visits were shorter.

There is a theory, said Aunt Tizzy, licking her dessert fork, that a father and his son never truly get along.

Mr. Eliot regarded his sister with disdain. Nat and I got along with Father splendidly, he said.

It was hard to imagine Uncle Nat's disagreeing with anyone. He was a bland, forgetful fellow with a squeaky voice, married to horsy Aunt Peg who looked like a man.

You, of course, are the exception to the rule, said Aunt Tizzy, winking at Lilian.

The Henderson girl ran off with a fellow from Connecticut, said Mrs. Eliot from down at her end.

The news was greeted with a gaping stillness; no one especially cared.

Is that Isa's daughter? said Aunt Tizzy finally. Though she no longer lived in Boston, she still knew the families.

That's right, said Mrs. Eliot. I always thought her a sensible girl.

Sometimes, said Aunt Tizzy with the air of one who knows more of the world than the others present, a girl who is not an idiot can behave like one, given the right situation and the right boy.

Why isn't this gossip? Lilian said.

Matter of general interest, said Mrs. Eliot.

There's no reason a son cannot be polite to his father, said Mr. Eliot. No reason in the world.

Errant genes, said Aunt Tizzy. Must be.

Yes, said Mrs. Eliot. I've often wondered how you and Edward could have turned out so differently. She smiled.

Lilian, however, had heard the explanation from her mother. It was from living with those cousins in Dover and not having them look after her which made Aunt Tizzy wild.

Tizzy Eliot's face hardened. Just one of those mysteries, I guess.

Mr. Eliot pushed back his chair with a short movement and placed his folded napkin square to his plate. Life is one grand mystery, he said.

Though Lilian had not seen him behave as if it were the least mysterious at all.

Lime street had always been a dreary narrow little street to Lilian, but as she turned the corner now in the brittle night it took on an august and dazzling cast. Walter Vail was there.

She felt that here was a new life, teeming with possibility, something all her own. She smiled the way people do alone on a street, unable to contain their joy. She arrived at the number he'd told her and lifted the knocker. He opened the door, holding a finger to his lips, and stepped back to let her in. His white shirt was luminous in the gloom.

Inside was quiet. His parents had spent the evening packing and were in bed. They had an early departure in the morning. Had they been Bostonian parents they'd have been downstairs to greet their son's guest, but being from New York, Lilian supposed, they had other priorities. Quite right, she thought. The day after Christmas Walter Vail was sailing. The fact of his going was always present, a fat stubborn thing in the corner, with arms folded, waiting.

The hallway had a spicy smell, Christmas cards were piled loosely on the hall table. Walter Vail led her without looking back up one flight of stairs, up the red and blue rug, then onto the rugs in the hall with wooden floor on either side. The house was dark and silent. They did not speak.

He led her into the shadowy parlor. Light from a sconce in the hallway threw a widening band of yellow over the floor. They stood near a window seat. Bells jingled on a carriage passing beneath them.

I missed you, he said. She saw his nervousness, but saw, too, that it was shallow. He put one arm around her, and she closed her eyes, leaning forward, and felt his lips on her temple. She stood this way for some time with a blissful expression. Eventually he pulled her to his chest, pressing her cheek against the button of his pocket. For a moment it occurred to her how free she was being. She hardly knew this man. But the war had changed things, and normal time was not the same. Leaning against him she felt nothing could disturb her happiness, but then she thought of the war and saw the round thing implacable in the corner and remembered.

How was dinner? she whispered.

Fine.

Did you . . . ?

I don't want to talk about it, he said. I feel bad for her.

I don't, Lilian said, and burrowed against him.

He ran his hand over her hair and tipped her head back. His face was grey in the window's light.

She had many questions for him, but wanted to show that she trusted him, and didn't say a word. She would have liked to tell him things — that she would wait, that her life was stretching out and she saw him in it. Of course she did not dare. She remembered Dolly's warnings and thought of all her mother had told her. Resting her cheek on Walter Vail's chest, it was hard not to feel that all the advice she'd been given and the warnings she'd heard were for girls other than herself and applied to boys other than Walter Vail. Boys, when you got up close, were quite different from the picture Mrs. Eliot or even Dolly Cushing painted. Boys did not care in the least if your fingernails were polished or if your hair was brushed. In fact, Walter Vail seemed to feel oppositely. She liked thinking of him and of how he was different from other boys. He seemed so clear about what he wanted, he did not falter.

These thoughts drifted as unformed clouds through Lilian's head. She had slipped into a dizzy repose — somehow they'd gotten onto the window seat — and was reclining beside Walter Vail who had propped up a pillow behind them. His voice rumbled through his torso, reverberating against her ear. He was asking her — she looked up — in a gentle voice, and her heart rose hearing it, if she wanted to take off her coat — she still had the heavy thing on! — so he could feel her more closely this one last time.

Having felt a great change in herself, Lilian no longer confided in Dolly Cushing and reserved her outpouring for the more discreet Jane Olney.

Jane had returned from Florida no more tan than when she'd left. She was a bony girl who dressed in simple linen shirts and wore her hair in a tattered bun atop her head. She often held a book loosely in one hand and directed her attention to it when her interest in the general conversation lagged. Lilian told her about the evenings with Walter Vail, finding new things in the retelling. *I'll never forget* floated inside her and she felt that with those evenings added to her she was more than she'd been before. Jane sat and listened without once telling Lilian what she ought to have done.

What an exciting time you've had, she said. He sounds like a lucky fellow.

They were walking around the Olneys' pond in Brookline. Lilian would be spending the night as she often did.

He did have a way about him, Lilian said, stepping in the snow, not the least aware that the canvas on her uppers was wet through.

* * *

{ 61 }

Some days before lunch she made the awful time pleasant by writing Walter Vail. She wrote on her tilted writing desk or took paper outside on the terrace despite the bitter air. She wrote less than she would have liked, not wanting to bombard him. Still, she figured many letters wouldn't reach him. She addressed him Dear Walter and signed herself Yours, Lilian. She tried to be amusing — soldiers would want to hear of gay things.

She received one letter from him and memorized every word. The letter did not strike as many personal notes as she would have liked, but then he was in a war.

March 17, 1918
Dear Lilian,

I am here in Rheims where you had told me of the cathedral and I wanted to let you know what has become of it. The town is awfully blown up. The streets are full of shell holes and the townspeople go about setting off the 'duds' stuck in the walls, ruining things further. I saw a picture of the cathedral in a book someone had last week and from the front I could imagine how it looked before its injury. Some of the front carvings up to thirty feet were saved by the sandbags and the clock had been removed for safety. One can still see the colored glazes. But up close you see the back and the sides which have been badly blasted and destroyed and much of the roof has fallen through. The ribs of one chapel roof still stand like a whale skeleton. I received a few fragments of red and blue glass and the guide who gave them to me said that often people shed a tear. I suppose I looked unmoved.

Many shells had burst inside and people were sorting

through the fragments. An old Roman gate still stood and some statues as well. I saw a bearded, wise-looking man put a head together. That's what has become of the cathedral. I remember your having admired it.

If you were here you would jump over the ditches and climb the barbed wire, not like the rest of us sad tired fellows.

Yours,
Walter Vail

II

Walter Vail

THE WAR was over, but Walter Vail did not return.
He had not been wounded, Lilian knew, and he certainly had not been killed — the Fenwicks would have known right away. He had simply not come back when the others did.

Lilian saw Madelaine Fenwick now and then but was not about to ask her for news of Walter Vail. The chill coming off Madelaine Fenwick threatened to contaminate her feeling. Lilian enlisted Dolly Cushing to find out something from the Nobles who sometimes saw Mrs. Vail's brother. All the information Burt Noble had was that Walter Vail had volunteered to stay overseas. Was he planning to return? Burt Noble didn't know. Burt had been over there himself at the end of the war and knew that some boys went a little strange after what they'd seen — Bud Sears still hadn't spoken since he'd gotten back, and Fellowes Moore had picked up a twitch. Hadn't Walter Vail been one of the fellows who'd been in the Rhine Valley? Yes, that was right, and Burt Noble knew there'd been some awfully bad things went on there.

Lilian shuddered to imagine.

Once she sat down to write Walter Vail's parents and in

the middle of the stiff and formal letter reflected how little Walter Vail had told her about them. It was likely he'd not told them a thing about her. She put the paper away.

A strange foreboding began to creep into her usual musings. Where once she had feared for Walter Vail's safety and was concerned for his morale, she now grew nervous about her place in his affections. Might he have forgotten her? Perhaps his tastes had reverted to Nita Russell. She flushed, and in doubting him, it was as if she were doubting her own feeling. She was still young enough to believe that depth of feeling made something true. And yet, the strange uneasiness grew, too unformed to put her finger on, too frightening to articulate. She tried to focus on her feelings for him, on how splendid he was, on how happy they would be. She created long, complex scenarios which involved arriving trains and understanding gazes. She thought of what a compelling figure he had cut, not like anything she'd ever seen. But then, perhaps he was *too* compelling for her. Surveying her memories, she dwelt on his kisses, and the trepidation passed. She knew that nothing as sweet as that could ever be bad.

That fall Jane Olney heard from Emmett Smith, who had it from his cousin, that Walter Vail was doing settlement work in Paris, helping families displaced by the war. Was there an address? Jane went directly to the cousin but just missed her — she'd gone on a trip to Virginia. When the cousin returned some time later, she had to get the address from a friend of hers, and by the time Lilian got it, it was the new year and months had gone by and there was some question as to whether the address was still good.

She felt joy as she wrote, but it was mixed with new fear. Would he want to hear from her? She'd not seen him in over a year. Perhaps he wanted to forget everything before the war. Or he was terribly busy, not the sort of person who wrote letters much. She had to admit she didn't really know what sort of person he actually was. She wondered how badly the war had affected him. She wrote him a cheery letter, the letter of a good clear Boston girl. She sent it in February. In late April she had heard nothing.

One day at the Fenwicks' for tea, Madelaine Fenwick mentioned in her bored way that the Vails had gone to see Walter in Paris and that according to them he had become quite *parisien*. He was thinking of writing a book about some aspect of French architecture.

Lilian, trying for the offhand, asked if he were still living at rue des Grands-Augustins and Madelaine stood up, not in the least curious why Lilian would want to know, and came back with a blue air mail envelope. Lilian looked at it as if an ancient relic had been unveiled. Madelaine languidly perused the envelope, looked inside at the small pages. Yes, she said, number fourteen, rue des Grands-Augustins. That was it. Then she cast a curious glance at Lilian.

Lilian mumbled something about a friend's having seen him in Paris and leaned forward for more tea.

How is the old charmer? said Dolly Cushing. Not hearing a great deal from Lilian, she assumed the infatuation had passed. He was naughty, wasn't he?

Lilian thought about this comment later and wondered about Dolly Cushing's contact.

Madelaine shrugged. I suppose so, she said. Though I

never saw the attraction. He's amusing but I could never imagine being interested in him that way. She looked idly at the letter, let it drop on the table. Lilian considered how if it were in her hands she would have it pressed to her breast.

She could only assume, then, that Walter Vail had gotten her letter and chose not to reply.

She was sick over it. She sat with Jane by the pond and threw stones into it, growing morose. Lilian no longer had the same proud feeling of love for him. It had slipped toward embarrassment. Was it the war which had changed him? Look at the Searses' hardly recognizing their son Bud or how when you got close you saw that Charlie Sprague shook. Maybe it was the war. Jane supported this theory. In that case, Lilian was the first to understand — she was an understanding girl.

Her mind went round and round, believing in him one moment, mortified the next. The worst thing was not knowing, she thought, but then, she still had hope.

IT WAS the end of life for her. I am dead, she thought. I will continue to walk through life but will be dead, sober and unscathed, because nothing will ever touch me again. I will be a spinster with a bun, wearing the same coat with a loose hem . . . No one would reach her as Walter Vail had done. No one would twist the button of her glove, speaking to her in the way he had, checking the expression of her face as if he knew what lay behind it. What went on in his head Lilian hadn't a clue, though she was sure it consisted of the most compelling stuff.

Some days she longed for company, others she wanted only to be left alone. She would have gone away, only she realized that wherever she went, her self would have to come with her.

The few days replayed themselves to her, unraveling like foil, flashing out bits. There was a dark bar shadowing his eyes, she felt his arm pressed across her middle, stopping her breath. She thought of questions she would have liked to ask him — they'd not occurred to her at the time — where had her mind been? Then the details grew menacing: his face was turned away, he was dining with Nita Russell, their heads close together. She watched her own careful feeling evaporate. What had been sweet to her apparently left no trace in him whatsoever.

She did not curse him, or tear up his letter, or speak badly of him to others. She'd seen other girls display a sort of amnesia about the boys they'd liked. Marian Lockwood and Chip Cunningham had been together for years and after she broke it off, Marian spoke so disparagingly of Chip, one wondered what she had liked about him in the first place. Madelaine Fenwick mentioned her old beau and shivered as if a goose were walking over her grave, and when Lilian asked Dolly Cushing what had become of the fellow from New Haven who used to travel back and forth on the express train to see her, she shrugged as if to say why would she know?

Of course the war had changed these things also. A lot of boys had not come back, and it made the ones who did different from everyone and the world around them different too. The life Lilian had known up till then was a fabric of generations: once, she had felt its monotonous pattern, but now she longed for the normalcy of it. She would not soon forget the terrible afternoons in the living rooms of the houses where a boy had not come home — the American flag on the iron balconies, the maids with red eyes.

The Lattimores had had an awful time with Richard Lattimore's dying just after the Armistice, not in battle, making the timing especially excruciating. Tommy Lattimore took on a different cast with the tragedy in his family. She walked with him one day along the river and Tommy did not once mention his brother, something Lilian quite understood.

She knew that things which once puzzled her could eventually dissolve over time. She used to wonder with some disturbance why the help were the ones who carried the dishes around the table while everyone else sat in their carved chairs. She'd wondered why Hildy's room was smaller than her own, or why she had never seen Rosie, who'd lived in the house longer than she, once sitting in the living room. Then, after living this way for a number of years and not knowing anything else, Lilian found herself taken aback when she came upon Rosie's niece out of uniform fixing her hair in the front hall mirror — anyone could have come by! She became annoyed when the gardener decided to trim the wisteria just as she brought guests to sit out back. As the wonder faded, the usual way of things took over. It happened in the same way evening happened, beginning with the balanced hour, half light, half shadow, then suddenly, imperceptibly, the light dims, it has become dulled, and one notices night has taken over.

But Lilian did not feel that time would alter her feelings about Walter Vail. That was quite beyond time.

THEY HAD come to New York for the wedding of their cousin Jock Baker to a New York girl, Esther Havemeyer.

The people were different in New York. Their clothes fit better, their faces were more masklike. The women wore roll-collared coats with narrow hips, shoes with higher heels, and cloche hats. The men were different too, but it was harder to say why, they held their chins a little higher so as not to miss anything going by.

It was impossible for Lilian not to think of Walter Vail. She received a vivid shock when she glanced out the window of their cab rattling down Fifth Avenue and saw a green awning jutting out over the sidewalk with 825 on it in white script — the Vails' address! Afterwards she felt she'd been given a drug and thoughts filled her like padding.

Aunt Tizzy was thrilled to have the Eliots visiting. The panels on her Persian coat flapped purposefully behind her as she led them down polished museum galleries and into red-upholstered restaurants. Mr. Eliot remained behind in the hotel and made appointments to meet with his law school betters. Aunt Tizzy pointed to buildings and listed the inhabitants, spouting names Lilian had vaguely heard of without the least idea of who they were.

. . . course when I was in Paris we ate these all the time. They're quite good here though not like the French make them . . . One must stay interested, Lil, it's the most important thing, don't you know? Interested in what's going on, course now it has to do with the vote. Imagine half the population not being able to vote. Let's hope it's different for you, Lil, that women will have *some* say. I've got my women's group working on it. Margaret, maybe you'd be interested in — ?

Mrs. Eliot sat by with one eyebrow raised, cautiously sampling the recommended gin fizzes, then gamely ordering another.

Well, maybe not, said Aunt Tizzy. Anyway, do you see that mural over there? She was his daughter-in-law. We used to come here with them when I first came to New York — funny little girl with a monkey face, never opened her mouth.

I'm sure she had her talents, said Arthur.

Aunt Tizzy slapped his arm, then made as if she were ignoring him. Mrs. Eliot did not seem to have heard.

The Havemeyer wedding reception was in a large round room surrounded by pillars wound with ivy and topped with a dome. Arthur danced with Lilian, surprising her with his dexterity. She was sitting at a gold-trimmed table eating yellow cake with Aunt Tizzy when a man with hair shiny as a dachshund's came over and joined them. Aunt Tizzy introduced him — he had a number of names and it took a moment to recite them — pressed her glove to his cheek, then, accepting an elderly man's invitation to dance, left him with Lilian. The man with the shiny hair leaned toward Lilian, giving off the smell of perfume.

Your aunt is a remarkable woman, he said. Unfortunately, there aren't many men strong enough to appreciate her.

Aunt Tizzy sailed by in the arms of the elderly man, her features suddenly taking on a strange new beauty, the greater for her not being aware of it.

Lilian regarded the man. Aunt Tizzy had been engaged once, to an Englishman, whom she'd brought home one Christmas. He had white hair and lips as red as liver. Once, when they thought they were unobserved, Lilian saw him spank her playfully on the bottom. But the wedding had not happened. Another woman intervened.

Perhaps she doesn't want to get married, Lilian said.

Every woman wants to get married, said the man. He sipped his champagne and watched with amusement as people passed. Why not?

Sometimes one doesn't find the right person, Lilian said, feeling awfully that she had, then had lost him.

One always does, said the man. People just don't always know how to do it is all.

People seem to, Lilian said.

Oh! the man said. I wasn't talking about *seeming*.

Lilian pushed at her cake.

You're not married, he said.

No, Lilian said, putting out her chin.

I love a pretty girl not married, the man said. She still has personality.

Lilian smiled.

He leaned forward conspiratorily. You know the bride and groom?

Jock's my second cousin. She I've only just met.

Handsome fellow, Jock. The man craned his neck for a glimpse, but didn't spot him anywhere. He shrugged. Shame she doesn't love him.

What?

The man spoke as if this were news everyone knew. She — well — doesn't love him.

How do you know?

Because, said the man pulling himself up to his full height. I believe she loves me.

Lilian regarded him with a slack mouth.

His eyes were merry, he winked at her. Sad for poor Jock, he said. Though Esther's an odd girl. He smiled broadly, thoroughly enjoying the spectacle the world had to offer. He said he was delighted to have met her and disappeared into the swaying crowd.

Who was that? said Mrs. Eliot.

A friend of Aunt Tizzy's, Lilian said with a look of wonder.

I should have known, said Mrs. Eliot. She shivered, and adjusted the lace fichu around her shoulders. Frightful fellow.

IT WAS over a year after Walter Vail had not come home
that Lilian was courted by a young man named Mike
Higbee. She knew she would have to go into the world
again and did, feeling dead, feeling also stronger with that
deadness since nothing mattered enough to hurt her.

Mike Higbee would arrive at the house, shake hands
heartily with Mr. Eliot, and compliment Mrs. Eliot on the
lacework smocking her dress — it was French, wasn't it?
He always arrived early, and would take Lilian to concerts
and shows and want to know her opinions. She had met
him with the Cunningham boys who were in the same club.
Mike Higbee was small with a broad back, he'd grown up
in Hanover, New Hampshire, and lived on Berkeley Street
in a basement apartment with two other law students like
himself.

Mike Higbee had an open, confident manner. He shook
his head at Lilian, marveling at her. He told her how beautiful she was in such a natural, normal way she wondered
what he was after. He had a thick hide and she found herself
saying things which the old Lilian would have found im-
polite.

How did you like the first act? Mike Higbee turned his

eager face to her. He withheld his opinions until she'd spoken.

Actually, I rather hate musical comedies.

How do you like my new jacket? Smart, eh?

I'm not partial to plaid.

To everything she said Mike Higbee exhibited amusement and admiration, and yet not seeming to hear her at all. It got on Lilian's nerves.

So what do you like best in a person? Mike Higbee grilled Lilian, preferring questions to statements.

I like that quality people have of seeing things in a fascinating way. She remembered Walter Vail's pointing out the odd way a passerby was walking or the wonderful archway on Pinckney Street. Each thing he'd singled out had taken on a particular, unusual quality.

With an eye, you mean, said Mike Higbee. He licked his lips thoughtfully, eyes ticking back and forth.

The next time they went out, a spring day boating on the Charles, Mike Higbee did not miss any opportunities to direct her attention to the many things which struck him.

He shook his head as one does at a coincidence. They were taking the tilted path down to the boathouse. *Déjeuner sur l'herbe!* he said. A little family group picnicking on the bank bore no resemblance whatsoever to Manet's painting. Mike Higbee checked Lilian's expression.

Lilian smiled politely, her social graces returning. The more she went out, the more she felt her boldness slipping from her and the old concern for convention returning. She had the feeling of being in a garden with a fence too high to see over.

Out on the water Mike Higbee waved toward Boston. Will you look at that? he said, controlling the tiller.

Lilian inclined her head. The clouds? The boats? The smokestacks? She was tired and perplexed.

Come on, he said. The view!

Ah, she said.

Mike Higbee nodded. Yes, he was getting the hang of it now. Lilian gazed down at the water moving glassily past the boat and wished she were in it, swimming away.

They walked through Harvard Square to a muffin shop he knew.

Great window, he said solemnly, indicating a nondescript brick building with a solitary square window in the attic floor. Lilian was unsure if he were addressing the fact of the window, its placement, or its shape, none of which was unusual.

At tea he pressed on, sensing nevertheless that he was losing ground. Suddenly he dropped all pretense and simply asked her why she didn't like him better.

She looked down at her broken, uneaten muffin and told him there had been another boy. She wasn't ready for a new one.

I'll wait, Mike Higbee said, and folded his short arms across his chest.

She who thought persistence an admirable trait here found it most annoying.

I don't think I'll ever be ready, she said.

And yet the moment she spoke of it a quiet pressure of hope moved through her and she saw for the first time there was a slight opening ahead — not with Mike Higbee — but with someone.

Mike Higbee, however, was seeing just the opposite, no hope at all. I'm sorry for that, he said, and his lower lip covered his upper one.

Not wanting to watch someone feel pain on her behalf, Lilian excused herself and took refuge for a short time in the ladies' lounge.

A T THE Crooks' garden party one saw the same people year after year. Dolly Cushing made sure to have a new hat for it, and Jane Olney simply changed the ribbon on her old one. Lilian wore a flower in her belt. The Crooks served the same lemonade, set out the same sliced beef, and put the round tables in the same places on the terrace. Everyone went out to Brookline for it. During the war with the scarcity of young men, the gathering was more like a ladies' tea party, more funereal than festive. Now, with the war over, there was relief and an air of sadness for the boys not home. The women stepped over the grass, sinking down in their heels, light dresses fluttering against their shins. The men rocked on their heels, and children jumped off the stone wall. Everyone was aware of the difference between the last time they'd tasted deviled eggs at the Crooks' and how it was now. Charlie Sprague was there on crutches, and Fellowes Moore still hadn't gained back the twenty pounds he'd lost. Everyone was especially conscious of the absence of Richard Lattimore who used to tie napkins in shapes for the children, and of Eleanor Crook's fiancé who had not made it back.

Lilian wandered down the tightly landscaped garden.

She saw Winn Finch sitting with his brother on a stone wall. He'd been a beau of Irene Minter's, not like her usual beaux. He stood up as Lilian came near.

I hear you're in medical school, Lilian said. Is it as nasty as they say?

Nastier, said Winn. His brother, whose name she couldn't remember, sat silently by.

Your father forcing you into it? said Lilian. Dr. Finch was a quiet, unassuming pediatrician.

Actually, he tried to talk me out of it, boomed Winn. He had a big person's loud voice and gestured with large hands. But there are too many doctors in my family — can't escape it.

The younger brother made no effort to join in the conversation, but sat there with his hands in his pockets, squinting up every now and then. His aloofness gave Lilian a peculiar feeling: she felt he was judging her. Perhaps the conversation was dull, but this was a party after all and if one weren't willing to converse then one shouldn't come. She didn't always want to make an effort, she might have preferred to sit quietly by, but one needn't be sour.

Later, she ate with Jane Olney, who was questioning with great earnestness in her deep level voice Mr. Crook's brother who was associated with U.S. Intelligence.

We heard you had great adventures over there, Jane said.

Mr. Crook had spilled some mustard on his front which swelled out like a barrel. It's mostly boring business, Mr. Crook said. Nothing for young ladies to be interested in.

Oh no, Jane said. I think it's fascinating.

Mr. Crook spooned ice cream into his spreading face,

then puffed on his cigar. More fascinating in books, I'm afraid. Lilian was having a difficult time picturing him as a spy. Behind him she saw the Finch brothers walking up the rise of the lawn. For a moment, it appeared the younger Finch was looking at her in a peculiar way.

Mr. Crook indicated his empty glass and heaved himself out of the chair.

Jane watched him go. Just imagine where he got that limp, she said.

Did you see Winn Finch? Lilian said.

I don't know, said Jane. She glanced down in her lap at the book she'd filched from the Crooks' study.

Do you know the brother? Lilian said.

Jane looked over to where the brothers were now at the bar, exchanging greetings with the spy Mr. Crook.

'Ve seen him, Jane said.

Something about him, Lilian said. Acts like he disapproves of you.

Since when do you know him? Jane said.

Since a minute ago. They laughed.

Near the end of the party some of the young people had drifted to the far side of the terrace and settled loosely around a table. Lilian sat on a garden bench beside Irene Minter who was carrying a parasol.

. . . it's just what happened to Wally Vail, said Emmett Smith with his usual authority.

A charge went through Lilian, turning her from solid into vapor.

I don't believe it, said the dark-haired girl with Chip Cunningham. Poor Chip continued to find girls who resembled Marian Lockwood — this one was petite too and had Marian's slight overbite.

True, Emmett Smith said. Despite his freckles and red hair, he carried an air of sophistication. Burt Noble's cousin saw them last week in New York. I'm surprised, Clare, you didn't know.

Lilian had never heard him called Wally. Perhaps they were talking about someone else.

He's back from France? said Tommy Lattimore. Tommy remembered him shipping over the same time as his brother, among other things. He looked in Lilian's direction. She was tucking at the sleeve of her dress.

He is, said Emmett Smith proudly.

I knew Wally growing up, said Clare. I can't at all picture him marrying a French woman.

Everything around Lilian seemed to stand out and pulsate.

Were they actually married or is it just the engagement? said Chip Cunningham, taking an interest because Clare did.

Already married, said Emmett Smith. He sniffed. That's what the scandal was, you see. The Vails had not been able to go to the wedding. It was small and quick — well, we know what that means.

The woman named Clare giggled at the back of her throat. Has he brought her back here? she said.

No, said Emmett Smith. They're staying in France. The wife doesn't speak English, and he's got that job now.

One of those lame jobs, said Tommy Lattimore, and his earlobes went red.

I would love to live in Paris, said Irene Minter dreamily.

He was such a flirt, that Wally Vail, said Clare. Her giggle was having a torturing effect on Chip Cunningham.

Lilian shut herself in the Crooks' downstairs bathroom, praying no one would find her. Running water in the sink, she didn't hear the soft knock. The door opened. It was that younger Finch brother, the one who'd looked at her in that ridiculous way.

I'm so sorry . . . His head ducked down, and he shut the door quickly.

The surprise brought Lilian back to herself. When she came out into the hall the Finch brother was still there, regarding her with the bold awkwardness of a child.

Are you all right? he said. I thought you might be . . .

No, said Lilian. I'm fine. She gave him a tight look and fled.

D OLLY CUSHING never exhibited a moment's depression until the day after she was married. She hadn't wanted the wedding to end.

Yes, Freddie Vernon was successful, people whispered in the pews of King's Chapel, but Freddie Vernon was also a jerk. At the reception he danced Dolly around, his eyes protruding to glimpse the important guests. He showed the same expression when surprised, or if someone offered an opinion which did not correspond with his own. Lilian had grown used to him, thinking that Dolly loved him, and had never seen evidence, though she did hear stories, of him snubbing those not in the Social Register.

Dolly was a fright to Freddie Vernon on their honeymoon till he got her on a camel; they rode out to the pyramids, and she felt herself again. She was the first of Lilian's intimates to marry.

Marian Lockwood came next, within the year, marrying Dickie Wiggin — lost Dickie who had the air of a man who's just missed his train. He was a dapper dresser, by Boston standards, always with a colorful bit of handkerchief in his pocket, wearing a straw boater in the spring. Marian led him about, happy to take charge. She always knew the smartest place to buy curtains and which florist had the biggest lilies. She was wonderful at spending money and Dickie Wiggin had a great deal of it. While Lilian could not imagine Marian's marrying a poor man, she did feel they genuinely liked one another.

Irene Minter was married after a short courtship to sporty Bobby Putnam, and soon after, seven months if anyone was counting, little Bobby was born. Lilian would have been more shocked if it had been any of the other girls, but Irene was different, and the usual rules did not apply. Bobby Putnam was fair-haired, white-teethed and rude to servants. When he wasn't playing golf, he was playing tennis or mixing drinks at the bar. He saw himself as a connoisseur of women and gave his expert opinion frequently.

Now that's what I call a looker — long-legged, big-boned, healthy, Bobby Putnam would say, listing attributes not possessed by his wife. And all the time Irene would gaze at him, enraptured, her black eyes stark in her pale face, stupefied by the sound of his voice and the look of him, not seeming to hear the sense of his words. And later, when the unhappiness started, she remained mystified about its cause.

Sister Cabot married Cap Sedgwick at the biggest wedding Boston had seen in a long time. The two of them strode towering up the aisle, leaning forward like giraffes.

At the reception at the Ritz-Carlton Lilian was approached by a tulle cloud of a woman smelling of perfume and squinting against her smile. I hear we have a friend in common, said Nita Russell. Have you heard any news of Mr. Vail?

Oh, Lilian said, not expecting to hear his name. No.

Me neither, said Nita Russell. Last I heard was about the baby.

Baby?

Little girl, yes. Didn't you know? But that was a couple of years ago, or maybe a year — I can't remember. Nita Russell looked lovely, the way people do who delight in and accept the ways of the world. He broke my heart, said Nita Russell brightly. He really did.

Lilian smiled weakly.

Said he was coming back for me after the war, and never did. She pouted, then shrugged, immediately putting it out of her mind.

I didn't know him that well, Lilian said.

Lucky for you, said Nita Russell and she gave Lilian's arm a pat.

Something stirred in Lilian — the old terror — and she felt another heavy curtain draw back, and found herself looking again at a different world — *said he was coming back for me after the war* — where the shadows were darker and the light was not a gentle thing.

A man carrying two glasses of champagne came up, handed one to Nita Russell, then looked agreeably at Lilian.

Oh, said Nita Russell, and she looped her arm in the man's. Have you met my fiancé?

THE DAYS went by as they always did in Maine. Lilian took a walk in the morning, had lunch with her mother and Arthur and a guest, then took another walk. Other activities included putting stuff in her hair, reading, shining her fingernails, and writing letters. Some days, they drove out with the cousins to Crabtree Point and stared at the hills across the Bay. One day they were fetched by Mrs. Bradley Parish's boat to look at an old house. It had three gardens and, they were told, a man's ghost inhabiting the gazebo. As they strolled down the bright paths, past the delphinium and the zinnias, Lilian had the feeling that he was nearby, she had an affinity for ghosts, and thought if she turned around, she'd see him so she did not turn around.

Another day, they returned from walking around Pierce's Pond to find the house reeking of garlic and the drinking water tinged with gin. Arthur said it was charming, if unusual. Aunt Tizzy had just arrived with her pyramid of luggage and in the morning they read the papers and were filled up with scandals among the best and most highly placed families. There were reading evenings and visits to the library by way of entertainment. For Aunt Tizzy's benefit, Lilian said she felt like the little poor girl living opposite the rich girl — watching Mrs. Amory's motor draw up in front of the Amorys' door every day to take her to lunch — though in truth, Lilian was thankful not to go out and meet anyone. Tommy Lattimore came nearly every day. He sat with her on the piazza with his long face, rearranging the large knuckles of his hand. He never spoke of his feelings for Lilian about which she was glad, having only a friendly regard for him. He was content to watch the comings and goings of the house, the cousins on the lawn, the gathering of raspberries, for there was not much activity at the Lattimores' house. Richard had been the most lively one there.

People were trying to forget about the war and to look forward. Some boys were still trickling home. Hardly any of the Island boys had come back — they'd all enlisted in the same regiments which had seen terrible casualties. Lilian had written Mrs. Cooper a note, saying how sorry she was about Forrey, and gave some money to the memorial fountain they were planning in the village center. Mrs. Cooper wrote back thank-you in a chicken scrawl and when they saw each other face to face on Main Street during the mail hour, they only smiled at each other and did not speak, having nothing more to say.

People had moved into the house next door so Lilian could no longer steal flowers or sit on the rocks. One of the new inhabitants whistled for the dog with two long notes, keeping it for too long a time, and Aunt Tizzy referred to him as the fiend. Lilian felt as if her life had been whittled down to a stick. The papers arrived a day late on the Island, and Lilian read them, drawn to the morbid news.

The Sedgwicks sailed through on their boat with Marian and Dickie Wiggin. They came to dine, bringing stories of the parties in Boston. Arthur maintained an aloof manner while they told of José Cutler's having nibbled the diamond earring off Amy Snow as they were dancing. Lilian tried to listen, but found it hard to take pleasure in the old things.

I'm reading a delightful book about how nasty the Germans have always been, Arthur said.

Lot of those, I should think, said Dickie Wiggin, looking summery in a white linen suit.

Did you tell the children about the Northern Lights? said Mrs. Eliot, for whom the next generation would always be children.

Cap and I saw them last night! said Sis Sedgwick. She was a strapping girl who loved sports and the outdoors despite a complete lack of coordination. Weren't they marvelous?

I was dead to the world, said Marian Wiggin, wrapping her sweater more cozily around herself.

They may be out tonight, Lilian said. Arthur and I see them from the roof.

She'll fall one day and break her neck, said Mrs. Eliot. And I won't be the least surprised.

A husband would keep that from happening, said Marian Wiggin.

She's too ill-tempered for a husband, said Arthur, adjusting the columbine in his buttonhole.

Lilian gazed at him merrily. Far too, she said.

Oh, we'll find someone, said Marian with authority.

Lilian shuddered at the thought.

Best place to see the Northern Lights is out on the water,

said Cap Sedgwick. He was a soft-spoken lawyer who stooped in doorways and had been a great rower for Harvard. Sis was as proud of his modesty as she was of his prowess, both of which were considerable. We've got to get you out there, Lilian, he said.

Lilian said she'd love to go and was glad when the next morning opened to downpouring rain.

IT RAINED for a week, imitating the deluge. On the first good day they took the boat up Molly's River.

The lunch basket was set on the flat part of the rock. People settled themselves on blue cushions with their books, others removed their shoes and merely looked out over the snaking water. Mr. Eliot in his shirtsleeves adopted his vacation pose, draping his tie over one shoulder. He'd woken up that morning with a swelled-up arm and decided that a tarantula had bitten him. In the shade of the pines slumped the figure of the boathand.

Lilian stood at the rock's edge in a black bathing costume. The water beneath her was dark green. She watched the ripples on the surface, dark lines blending with lighter lines of reflected sky, and became thoughtful. She still longed for something, and told herself it wasn't Walter Vail. She tried to imagine being alone forever, like Aunt Tizzy, and thought, I can do it, but began to feel like a stone. If only she could meet a nice boy, she wouldn't care about anything else, just as long as he was honest and good and knew how to laugh and didn't have any airs. That was all she wanted. The tide was at its highest. She dove in.

How can she do that? said Mrs. Glover, a widow who

often accompanied the Eliots on their excursions. Her neck trembled as she shook her large head.

Mrs. Eliot, her back erect, turned and idly followed her daughter's form moving out in the water. A large hat cast shade over her, a summer throw lay on her lap. Lilian doesn't feel the cold, said Mrs. Eliot. Never has.

You know what they say about a girl who loves to swim, said Aunt Tizzy. She was dressed for the Riviera in a peacock and green bathing outfit with matching turban.

What's that? said Arthur, suffering visibly to be with his family.

Never mind, said Mrs. Eliot with a tight mouth. Mr. Eliot's attention remained directed at his book.

It means she loves to dance, doesn't it? said Mrs. Glover, looking baffled.

Among other things, murmured Aunt Tizzy. She tucked at her red hair.

I wonder if Tommy Lattimore loves to dance, said Arthur.

Doubt it, said Aunt Tizzy, returning his smirk. Her rouged cheeks stood out as vivid spots.

Tommy Lattimore is a very nice boy, said Mrs. Eliot, acting as if she were only half in the conversation. She'd come to agree with Mr. Eliot about the one during the war, the one from New York, not being good for Lilian.

Is this Lilian's beau? said Mrs. Glover. One does miss everything when one goes away.

Arthur shrugged. He comes every day, he said.

Mrs. Glover rustled. Are we talking about an engagement? She addressed the shaded figure of Margaret Eliot.

Lilian has not mentioned anything to me, Mrs. Eliot said.

And I can't imagine she will, said Aunt Tizzy. She signaled to Arthur and stood up, carrying her little purse, to slip around the cove for a cigarette. She'd promised her sister-in-law not to smoke in front of the children. Lil's a grand girl, she said. Tommy Lattimore is merely nice.

The Lattimores are a lovely family, said Mrs. Glover. They're just splendid people.

And they've had their misfortunes, said Mrs. Eliot, looking solemn.

Mrs. Glover nodded.

He didn't even die in the trenches, Arthur said. The guy got botulism.

The women glared at him. Arthur stood up and followed his aunt.

At first, the water took her breath away, then she got used to it and it was fine. It was nowhere near as cold as the water out in the Bay. She'd not been swimming in a week, and the water seemed to have a thickness to it from all the rain. Lilian kicked her legs beneath her, feeling the pressure on her knees, the swirling against her ankles. It pushed on her arms and made her fingers feel strangely webbed. She was buoyed up, the cold water sparkled around her.

It would never do with Tommy Lattimore, she knew that. He was sweet, but there was something she was after that would never come from him. She could not have said what the something was and felt silly not being able to

articulate it. Her father would say if there were no words
for it, it did not exist.

She swam through a narrow between two outcroppings
of white rock. To the right she saw Aunt Tizzy leaning
back against a chaiselike rock and Arthur higher up,
hunched over like a griffin. Smoke issued forth from both
of them. They waved in a lazy way. She swam past.

At the end of an inlet she saw a house half-hidden by
elms. A group of apple trees dotted the slope leading down
to the shore where, out on the water, a white sloop was
anchored. A man appeared on deck bare-chested and
walked up to the bow. He fiddled with some cleats and
ropes, unwinding a halyard from a wire stay. A woman's
head rose from the cockpit. Her hair was cut in a bob and
her neck was tan. She called to the man, then stepped out
on deck. She was wearing a pale Japanese robe which
flapped around her knees, a sort of dressing gown. She
brushed back the hair from one eye as she stood nearby
watching the man. Suddenly she leapt backwards — the
man had sprung up after her. He caught hold of her shoulders and the two of them wrestled against the rope railing,
laughing, and after a struggle, the man's feet were up in
the air and then disappeared over the side. It was a moment
before Lilian heard the muffled splash.

The woman braced herself on the railing, back arched,
and rocked side to side. The sound of laughing and splash-
ing awoke in Lilian a feeling she'd not had in a long time.
There was life where these two were — quite different from
the life back on the picnic rock. Lilian had once felt so ready
for life — then Walter Vail had happened to her and after-

wards she no longer felt so ready. She thought, But if I were on that boat . . .

The man swam around to the side of the boat where a rope ladder dangled against the hull. Lilian got a peculiar, thrilled sensation to think he and she were in the same body of water. He climbed up the rungs, rounded into a threatening pose, and the woman's rippling figure darted up to the bow. The man stalked her, big and dripping. She cried out, and wound herself around a bow stay with both arms. The man took hold of her shoulders, she cried out again — he was all wet! He tugged at her, but not with real effort. She was pleading, laughing. Then, with one harsh yank, he pulled her away from the stay. She screamed a high-pitched scream — they could probably hear it around the bend in the river. The screaming stopped, and while the woman still tried to free her arms, she was speaking to the man in a lower, more reasonable voice.

He let her go and rested on one leg, waiting, arms crossed. The woman hesitated, then crumpled forward, folding around herself, down onto her knees — Lilian's heart beat, watching — then she crouched over completely and put her head to the deck and seemed to kiss the man's feet. Her face turned up to him. Their laughter had changed. She knelt up and put her hands on his hips. Her elbows stuck out to the side so the flap of her sleeves fluttered down. The man glanced around him, and for one dazzling moment Lilian thought he spotted her dark seal head in the water, but his gaze swept by like a lighthouse beam — he did not see anyone. He turned back to the woman below him, his chin down to his chest, and touched the top of her head, guiding it. The head had begun to move.

She turned and swam back to her family, feeling something close to hope within her.

Look at you, said Mrs. Glover, observing Lilian's dripping form. I should learn to go in. You look positively glowing.

Lilian went into the woods to change. As she toweled off, her skin white in the dappled pine shadow, she heard a woman's scream coming from the direction of the white boat. Then she heard a splash. It was not as large a splash as the one the man had made. Its effect was to stun Lilian. It was the woman's splash.

On the way back in the boat Lilian stared, facing the wind. Her mother was talking about having Mr. Francesco to dine and Mrs. Glover said her second cousin was married to his sister. Lilian felt hope dying in her. She tried to save some, and took what she could, tucking it away deep down for safekeeping, deciding not to look at it again for a long time.

III

Mrs. Eliot

FIVE YEARS passed and Lilian Eliot went on much as she had gone on before Walter Vail. Her friends were producing children. Dolly Vernon had two boys and Marian Wiggin two girls and Cap and Sis Sedgwick one of each. Irene Putnam had lost her second baby, a girl born dead, but was successful with the next try. Lilian went out frequently and was the object of considerable conjecture about when she would wed. It was the major thing which happened in a girl's life, after all. The thing had even happened to Jane Olney.

Jack Ives was a gruff fellow with a barrel chest. He was usually seen standing apart from the general conversation, looking at his feet, yet when asked a question frowned and gave an answer showing he'd been listening all along. He liked his Scotch, and he loved Jane. Shortly after meeting her he made friends with her family and when he took her out to parties he did not let go of her hand. Jane seemed not in the least surprised. She had been waiting patiently for a man to come along and now he had. They were married in Brookline in May 1924 with a yellow-striped tent on the Olneys' back lawn and not too many people. Arthur gave a toast about how he'd always admired Jane and everyone remarked on his eloquence. When it came time to throw the bouquet, a custom she and Lilian agreed was humiliating, Jane threw it into the pond.

At dinner one night Mrs. Eliot said, I met a nice boy at the Moores'. She looked pointedly at Lilian. Gilbert Finch I think he's called. He had a nice voice. I heard him talking to the children.

That the doctor's son? said Mr. Eliot, not especially interested. He had one fist on the table. Think I was at school with him.

There are two sons, Lilian said. One's a doctor, too.

Which was the one threw over Irene Minter? said Arthur.

How can you remember that? Lilian said. It was ages ago.

One doesn't forget Irene Minter. She has atrocious taste in men. Arthur made a dramatic gesture. Anyone who marries Bobby Putnam —

No gossip at the table, Mr. Eliot said.

Mrs. Eliot took three short sips of her wine before replacing the glass on the table. We're not maligning anyone, Pa, she said.

I hardly consider it complimentary to be labeled as someone who — how did Arthur so colorfully put it? — threw over Irene Minter. The girl is not a javelin.

Arthur burst into laughter.

Mrs. Eliot smiled with an expectant look, waiting for whatever was funny to drift over her way and make her laugh, too.

That was the older one, Winn, Lilian said without enthusiasm. We were talking about Gilbert.

She'd learned his name in the five years since he'd looked at her at the Crooks' garden party. She saw him now and then, across the street at the Fourth of July parade, hidden in a hat, or down at the end of a long yellow porch at the Lorings' Labor Day tea. He'd been at Eleanor Crook's wedding to Charlie Sprague; she'd noticed him loitering out in the driveway with the chauffeurs. She had read something about him somewhere, oh yes, in her father's *Harvard Alumni Magazine* in an article about curling. Curling!

He must prefer talking to children over adults, Lilian said. I've never heard him utter more than two words.

He seemed to have a lot to say to Nita Russell, Mrs. Eliot said. Though I guess she's Bancroft now, even though . . .

What was she doing there? Lilian said.

Ada Amory says she's moved home, said Mrs. Eliot.

Was that the unfortunate . . . ? Mr. Eliot frowned over his potatoes.

Yes, said Mrs. Eliot.

There was a pause in the conversation.

Arthur said, I liked Jim Bancroft. He was wild.

And look where it got him, said Mrs. Eliot. He was driving that boat too fast anyway.

I'm surprised she's come back to Boston, Lilian said.

Very sweet girl, said Mrs. Eliot. Anyway, he asked after you.

Who did?

Gilbert Finch.

He asked after me? Lilian recalled the strange pale eyes, and how they'd looked at her without embarrassment.

I had to ask Sally Kimball who he was. I get those young people so confused.

What did he say?

Who?

Gilbert Finch!

He said, hello, Mrs. Eliot, how's Lilian?

And what did you say?

Very well, thank you. I didn't know who he was.

And then what did he say?

Fascinating conversation, Arthur said.

You know, I just don't remember, said Mrs. Eliot.

Lilian mumbled, He was just being polite.

Something the whole table might like to hear? boomed Mr. Eliot.

Lilian stuck out her chin.

Sally Kimball seemed to think he'd had some trouble with, you know, in the war. Mrs. Eliot anchored her glass while Patrick poured more wine. Mr. Eliot had conceded to bootleg after a long coolness on Mrs. Eliot's part, but restricted the alcohol to the dinner table.

Welcome to the club, said Arthur though he'd not been a member. He indicated to Patrick with a grand smile to keep pouring in his glass.

What's he doing these days? Lilian said.

Who? Mrs. Eliot smiled down at her plate.

Gilbert Finch. Lilian found it odd to say his name.

Working somewhere I suppose, said Mrs. Eliot.

Hear that, Arthur? Mr. Eliot rarely looked at his son directly and did not now. This fellow has a job.

Poor devil, said Arthur.

SEVEN MONTHS later Lilian and Gilbert Finch announced their engagement. It happened in the following way.

He was at the Cunninghams' Christmas party. Lilian
supposed he had been there other years, but she'd not noticed him then. He handed her a glass of eggnog as she
stood with Beany Sprague and excused himself to deliver
drinks to his aunt. Irene Putnam's little Bobby came over
to show her a cookie in the shape of a snowman, and before
she knew it, she was surrounded by children. Contrary to
Mrs. Eliot's report, Gilbert Finch did not appear particularly anxious to talk to her.

After New Year's the Sedgwicks had a dinner party and
seated Lilian next to Gilbert Finch. They had a nice chat
about dogs and January and Agatha Christie, about which
they were both fond. She noticed that he ate everything on
his plate but the green vegetables, like a child. But for
coffee the men stayed forever in the dining room discussing
politics, a new interest of Cap's.

Later that month, Lilian and Tommy Lattimore went
with Marian and Dickie Wiggin to the moving pictures,
and Dickie brought along Gilbert Finch whom he'd known

from St. Mark's. Lilian sat between the two single men and watched the movie cartoon of Hermann the Great Mouse, enjoying it more than she would have thought. Marian nearly had hysterics laughing, enthralled by such moments as the stove's walking across the room and lifting the kettle off itself with its pipe. Lilian was sorry when Gilbert Finch declined to join them afterwards for dessert.

One Friday afternoon Lilian was walking with Nathaniel Weeks, a young man who volunteered with her at the hospital. Sometimes at the end of the day they would go window shopping on Newbury Street and Nathaniel Weeks, who had money, would try to get Lilian to say what she liked so he could buy something for her. She was not sure she wanted anything from Nathaniel Weeks. As they crossed the Common, they ran into Gilbert Finch on his way to North Station. A binocular case hung against his chest and he carried the smallest overnight bag Lilian had ever seen. He stood very still as if waiting for Lilian and Nathaniel Weeks to release him. His clothes were loose on his solid body, the collar crimped at the back, his sleeves baggy at the elbows, but somehow the disarray suited him. He was spending the weekend on the North Shore but didn't say whom with. Nathaniel Weeks began to discuss a favorite topic, the weather. Lilian managed to ask about the binoculars.

I like to look at birds, said Gilbert Finch.

Nathaniel Weeks tried to make a pun about his name which didn't come off, but all three laughed politely.

Lilian noticed that Gilbert Finch's full upper lip looked as if someone had punched him, or as if he were holding back tears. One ear angled out from his head, pointing slightly, elfin. His eyes were pale with dark lids below as well as above, giving him the air of having felt sorrows. Lilian remembered hearing his mother had died when he was eleven or twelve.

As he ran to his train, he took a course off the paths, moving with an athlete's grace. It occurred to Lilian how whenever she saw Gilbert Finch he was alone.

Imagine looking at birds in the middle of winter, Nathaniel Weeks snorted. He had on polished shoes and a pressed scarf. Beneath his hat, his hair was slicked back with a center part like the other fellows'.

I think it's a splendid idea, Lilian said.

In the following months Lilian accepted invitations she would once have found excuses for, hoping in a dim way for a glimpse of Gilbert Finch. She was not more interested in him than in any other boy, but there was something about his quiet reserved way, and he had asked about her that time. She just wondered what he was like. But Gilbert Finch did not go out so much. She planned things with Marian and Dickie Wiggin, hoping they would ask Gilbert Finch along. Marian, who was forever proposing different fellows for Lilian, took no hint when it came to Gilbert Finch. Gilbert's a little lost, was all Marian said.

Downtown one day on her way to buy ribbon, Lilian ran into him, Gilbert Finch, his hair mussed, carrying a crumpled newspaper. She felt she could have talked to him for a long time, and yet was unable to come up with the first word to get started. Out of nowhere Freddie Vernon appeared like a steam engine, exclaiming that Dolly was just around the corner, and if Lilian hurried she could catch her on Exeter Street, then he turned to Gilbert — he was damned interested in the work Finch was doing, why didn't they have lunch sometime? — leaving Lilian with nothing to do but say good-bye and be on her way.

In March when the mist hung over puddles in the street, Gilbert Finch got sick and took to his bed. There was a bad influenza going around — with some fatalities among the poor — but according to Dickie Wiggin that wasn't what was wrong with Gilbert Finch. Dickie explained deliberately one day at tea, straightening his pants' crease, peaking his handkerchief, that Gilbert Finch, though athletic, had always been prone to illness. Why, he'd missed a whole winter at St. Mark's, and had to make it up at summer school to graduate. Emmett Smith, taking up his tea saucer, began telling stories about Paris where he'd just come back from, but Lilian only half-listened to the chatter which once had made her mouth water. She did not care a bit. She was far more interested with what went on at 242 Marlborough Street where a certain someone resided.

She would have liked to go visit him but didn't know him well enough and was sure he would think it odd. Marian and Dickie did go, and said that Gilbert Finch had asked them to say hello to their friend Lilian Eliot, which she thought was friendly of him, more friendly really than he ever was to her face.

The next time Lilian saw him was at Dickie Wiggin's birthday party a few weeks later. A strange feeling gathered in her as she dressed in a new pink blouse, knowing that Gilbert Finch would be there, and by the time she walked up the steps to the Wiggins' house the feeling had grown into a disturbance. She wondered, as she walked in the door, if it showed.

She glimpsed him across the room — he looked thinner and younger — and went straight for the bootleg, though she hardly liked to drink, and had one. She thought, I'm quite used to boys, what is it about this Gilbert Finch of all people?

Finally she went up to say hello, her face smooth and friendly, betraying nothing of her disturbance. I'm glad to see you're better, she said.

He checked over her shoulder, as if to see whom she was with. Lilian found herself flattered.

The curling team must have missed you, she said.

You're not a follower of curling, he said.

No, but I read about it. You're quite famous, aren't you?

He was wearing a brown wool jacket with a rumpled lapel. He looked at her curiously. Been buying any ribbon lately? he said.

No. She smiled and felt herself flush. I've been making do with what I have.

I'm sure you have no trouble with that, he said.

Oh, he was better than she'd thought.

If you're ever buying ribbon again —

Yes?

Well, sometime you might —

But he was interrupted by Marian Wiggin's bustling up to them and announcing that they had to come into the other room to hear the wonderful Victrola she'd bought Dickie for his birthday. Everyone sat and listened while she played one of the new songs, but no one got up to dance.

How is your young man? Mrs. Eliot said, bringing a small vase of daffodils into Lilian's room.

He's not my young man, Lilian said.

Mrs. Eliot lifted one eyebrow.

He's not, Lilian said.

Since Dickie Wiggin's birthday she'd seen him exactly twice. Once when she'd gone with Marian and Dickie to see their house in Beverly Farms and Gilbert Finch had come along. They motored out on a fine April day and walked through the chilly rooms draped with white sheets. It was warmer outside and they lay on the beach without their coats and shoes and ate sandwiches the cook had made. Gilbert Finch knew all the names of the birds, hardly having to look. He was able to tell a bufflehead from a tiny speck dipping between waves. Lilian discovered that he was the sort of fellow who moves over on a bench to make room for a girl, not thinking that the girl might want to sit close.

You've been awfully irritable lately, Mrs. Eliot said. She'd pass Lilian's door and see her sitting with a book, not reading, staring.

He doesn't like me that way, Lilian said. Which is fine

with me. Gilbert Finch was hardly the sort of fellow she pictured marrying. Still, she was oddly happy in his company and when she didn't see him would become unaccountably sad, with his face in her mind.

No need to shout, Mrs. Eliot said and closed the door.

The second time she saw him was for lunch downtown. She'd mentioned she needed new ribbon and he took the hint. They didn't go to a fancy place, but to one where they carried their plates from the bar to a little banquette. Lilian knew he was shy, but couldn't get rid of the feeling that he did not seem to care if she were there or not. At moments, he seemed to be eating alone.

Afterwards he'd taken her up to the Athenaeum — he had a few minutes before getting back to the office of the shipping company — where they looked at portraits of his ancestors. Some of them were buried down the hill in back of King's Chapel where some of Lilian's relatives also resided. Judge Henry Gilbert Finch had pounded the gavel on display in the Old State House, the oldest gavel in the country. They stood in a marbled doorway of the Athenaeum looking into a reading area and saw a girl lift the pad of paper on which she'd been writing and kiss the bottom of the page. Lilian turned to Gilbert to catch his eye, but turned away not wanting to embarrass him. That he was blushing terribly she felt was a good sign.

S HE INVITED him to tea. He stood in the doorway
when she opened it, holding a brown hat in his large
soft hands. His coat was buttoned irregularly over a vest.
He smiled without showing his teeth.

Lilian led him in, took his hat to the library, and brought
him into the living room.

Pa, this is Gilbert Finch and, Ma, I think you've met?

Gilbert Finch shook their hands naturally.

Mrs. Eliot regarded him with confusion. Why, certainly,
she said with a scattered look.

Knew your old man in school, Mr. Eliot said. Behind
me.

Mr. and Mrs. Eliot were using the different voice reserved for people outside the family.

Tea? Lilian said.

They sat down. Gilbert Finch sat on the leather-cush-
ioned guard in front of the fireplace, a spot usually taken by
children. He stretched his legs out in front of him, showing
his socks, balancing on his heels.

Mrs. Eliot smiled doubtfully. Mr. Eliot patted his watch
pocket. Lilian felt Gilbert Finch's pale gaze. She poured tea
past a cup's brim, drained it from the saucer, and fumbled

with sugar tongs. The finer strands of her dark hair had loosened and were wreathed into a sort of web. No bones showed in her full face making her look younger than her twenty-six years. Her chin was slightly cleft, her lips were pursed.

Was surprised to see he'd become a doctor, Mr. Eliot said. Gilbert Finch looked at him blankly. Your father, I mean.

Gilbert Finch saw no reason to respond.

That is, Mr. Eliot went on. Always getting into mischief, your father. He let out a gruff laugh.

I can see how one might think that's a surprise, said Gilbert Finch. He regarded Mr. Eliot with such a clear pale look that Lilian found her father looking muddled and, even more astonishing to the daughter, foolish.

Lilian handed Gilbert Finch a cup.

I thank you, he said, turning his gaze to her. Whatever he looked at seemed to hold him rapt, and the thing itself took on a fascinating aspect. He sipped his tea, feet upright across the parlor rug, seeming not to have a care in the world.

Lilian got him to talk about his bird-watching, relieving some of the tension. Mr. Eliot nodded his head, having respect for the pastime, and Mrs. Eliot held her teacup at chest level, signifying interest.

Shore birds were his favorite. They were the most delicate and beautiful. He'd seen an Arctic gull this winter — very rare — blown down in a storm. He'd spotted it huddled with the other gulls out at Tuck's Point in Manchester.

We see lots of pheasants out at Mr. Eliot's brother's in Brookline, said Mrs. Eliot. They pop right out of the woods.

An Asian bird, bellowed Mr. Eliot with authority.

That's right, said Gilbert Finch, dismissing it. Pheasants fell into the same category as robins and blue jays, crows and herring gulls, birds not worth noticing. Bird watchers were more interested in songbirds or migratory birds, especially if they were indistinguishable and brown.

After Gilbert Finch was gone, Mr. Eliot headed out to the back yard to check for spring shoots. Agreeable fellow, he said with a frown.

Mrs. Eliot sat back a little on the sofa. That was your Gilbert Finch? Then I wonder who the boy was at the Moores', she said. I've never seen this fellow before in my life.

IN EARLY JUNE Lilian sat on the steps of the veranda of the Wiggins' house in Beverly Farms, looking down toward the rocks where Gilbert Finch and Dickie Wiggin were fishing. They'd been at it a long time, and Lilian had been watching as long, having brought out her woolwork — something for Dolly Vernon's little boy, her third — only to botch up stitches and have to unravel. She felt she could have sat on that step and watched and watched.

That morning she and Gilbert Finch had walked to the point, hanging back from the others, and now she went over the different things he'd said. He talked about a trip he'd taken to California, riding horses through the hills and sleeping on the ground, and while it was not something Lilian was usually interested in, she found she couldn't hear enough about it. It was fascinating. He talked about his job at the import company, and she pictured him in his office with his jacket off and his shirtsleeves bunched up as she'd seen him that day in town. Marian had told her he worked with a charity which placed young boys in homes after reform school, and she'd pressed him about it, admiring his reticence.

She watched his back down below with the sheen of the

late afternoon water behind him and felt something fan through her like a warm wind. He pulled in his line and examined some kelp or seaweed around the hook. He crouched down to study it. His focus gave a sort of honor to the hook, to the whole activity of fishing! To think this was the same man who probably had stood near the plate of molasses cookies at the Morses' on any number of Tuesday evenings, the same fellow she'd probably skated by a hundred times on winter afternoons at the pond — and she'd not even noticed him!

It seemed impossible. He looked to her now the most remarkable person she'd ever seen.

Her attention, tight and elastic, stretched down to where the men were fishing. She looked at his rumpled figure in a white shirt — he wore a hat with a collapsed brim — and saw an aura around him of — what was it? — goodness. Now that she thought about it, she realized there had always been something about him before, she'd just not thought of it in the right way. He was not a frivolous man. There was no self-importance in those arms, no inflated pride in that posture. He stood up and cast again, she could hear the faint whirring of the line. She glanced down at the little sweater and realized she'd gone too far with a row. Lilian had known the attentions of a frivolous man, and here in the shade with the smell of the sea wafting up to her, she could hardly remember what in it had appealed to her. The needles clicked listlessly as she knitted. She'd certainly paid a price for it. The effect of this was decidedly different. While she was reminded of the old feeling, the wonderful blurring at the edges, she found that in contemplating Gilbert Finch she was in a calm, familiar place. She was not changed into something other, like the impersonation she'd done with Walter Vail. She felt returned to herself.

Shall I have the cocktails brought out on the veranda? Marian called from an upper window, pausing in her bustle about the house. I think, why not? she answered herself, and her head popped back inside.

Lilian no longer wanted to run away or to be something different. What had she been thinking of? Looking back, amused, a little condescending, she saw an altogether younger person. A rather foolish one, at that. She was just a regular girl from Boston — how could she have expected to hold and to understand someone like Walter Vail? Of course, he would never have understood her either. Gathering in her was the sense that the man down on the rocks, the one she'd watched sit cross-legged on the beach, the one who carefully rolled his napkin into a sausage after dinner, was someone she could understand. And he could understand her. It was as if their ancestors' proximity in King's Chapel yard gave them a sort of affinity. That familiarity had once made her recoil — she smiled to herself — but now she saw the sense of it: instinctively, they knew one another. In these past few days she'd spent with him, she'd found she met herself, the girl she'd been long ago, the one Arthur would have sprayed with the garden hose or sat with up on the gabled roof.

Are they still fishing? Marian cried from the open hallway, moving at a fast clip toward the kitchen. She threw out questions like lines, not caring to reel them in.

What a a nice quiet way he had. His lack of self-aware-ness was so like a child's. Because of this she felt she could trust him thoroughly. He was certain, like a rock against this shore was certain, as solid as a brick in the sidewalk on Beacon Street. The day before they'd motored inland past the stables of Hamilton and the marshes of Ipswich and Gilbert Finch had sat near the window letting the wind blow on his face, enigmatic, at peace. Lilian had noticed that the boys who'd been abroad didn't talk about it much. Gilbert Finch had gotten to France only at the end of the war. He did say he didn't know how the other fellows had lasted so long. It was all she had heard him say on the subject.

Thinking of him, the warmth fanned through her again, stirring her dormant self, her real one. Her knitting needles lay, useless wooden sticks, on her lap. She stared down at him and fixed in her mind the notion that he would save her. Suddenly it was her last hope.

It was in this way, musing and alone, that Lilian Eliot decided her fate.

THE NIGHT he asked her to marry him was a June night in the back garden of Fairfield Street. There was a fog from the river. The light from the drawing room doors fell across them. Gilbert Finch held Lilian's hands in his own large soft ones. She had just said yes.

His feet moved on the gravel, releasing the smell of wet soil. May I kiss you?

A big kiss or a little kiss?

A little one, he said.

His lips were gentle and dry, and for a confused moment she was thrown back to a kiss of many years before, not so very far from where they now stood. His arm came around her, spreading warmth and as she moved closer to be surrounded by him, he mistook her movement, thinking she was shy, and drew back. He gave her cheek a little peck, then pecked her hair.

You're not scared of me, are you? she teased.

She had meant to put him at ease, but when she saw the confusion flooding his face, she wished she could have taken it back.

He embraced her, hiding his face. She couldn't remember anyone having needed her before. Tommy Lattimore had worshiped her. Mike Higbee had wanted to win her. And Walter Vail had wanted merely to sample her. Gilbert Finch was different. His eyes were closed. She touched his cheek, astonished at what seemed to be her power over him. It was greater than any power she'd ever felt, and came from a generous place.

He mumbled something she couldn't hear, and she drew back from the embrace to ask him what it was.

I never thought I'd have this, he said.

She lifted her chin — for another kiss — and saw his eyes welling up. He hid his face in her hair, overcome, and she thought, I've waited this long, there's no hurry, I've found him now.

They were to be married in late September. That summer Lilian had planned to take the grand tour with her family. They would spend the last of August in Maine as usual and Gilbert Finch could visit on the weekends from town.

Lilian received notes of congratulations. Winn Finch wrote that he thought his brother had made an inspired choice. Her new father-in-law sent her a three-page letter in tiny print welcoming her to the family and offered as a wedding gift her choice of anything in their house but his bed. Her friends were divided between those who simply said how happy they were and those who felt they could now admit how worried they'd been about her, feeling that now she was getting married any opinion concerning her previous twenty-seven years was of no further consequence.

In one way it was true. She no longer felt her birthday was September 11th but instead June 17th, the day he proposed.

She, who had always been skeptical of the joys of marriage, now passed beneath the adorned bower, sheepish at first then very quickly not caring a fig for the old way she'd thought. She was giddy and girlish discussing the wedding preparations. People remarked on the change in her. How original of her to choose Gilbert Finch, they said. They had expected an unusual choice, and it was the mere ordinariness of this which made it all the more unusual. They gazed now with new eyes on the bland, quiet figure of Gilbert Finch. He was, of course, pleased by the engagement, but if one were observing Gilbert Finch one would have detected no notable change in his behavior at all.

Bᴜᴛ ᴡʜᴀᴛ does he intend to do? Mr. Eliot said, cutting his meat with deliberation.

He doesn't *intend* to do anything, Pa.

Excuse me, Lilian. Mr. Eliot lifted his face like a blind man's, flabbergasted by his daughter's tone. I believe it is usual for a man to be concerned with his daughter's prospects.

Sorry.

What was that?

I said I'm sorry, Pa.

I should hope so. Mr. Eliot chewed solemnly. I repeat my question: what does the young man intend to do?

Right now he's working for the importing company . . .

I know that, Lilian. That much he has told me himself.

Dear, what Pa means is, what are his long-term plans? Mrs. Eliot had the unruffled manner she took on after her second cocktail.

He hasn't decided, Lilian said. He doesn't want to stay at the company forever.

Just what I'm getting at, said Mr. Eliot.

Whatever Gilbert does is fine with me, said Lilian. Anything he chooses to do . . .

Mr. Eliot murmured, Doesn't need to choose, marrying you.

What? Lilian dropped her fork.

Pa's just concerned about your future, said Mrs. Eliot. She smiled at the table, the picture of contentment.

I can speak for myself, Margaret.

Of course you can, dear.

Does Mr. Finch have any — ? Mr. Eliot began.

Arthur burst in breathlessly. Are we dissecting poor Gilbert? Well, I like him well enough. He's no lemon.

Thank you, Lilian said.

Where have you been? said Mr. Eliot, not glancing anywhere near Arthur's direction.

Oh, said Arthur with surprise, though his eyelids remained low, giving him a detached air, a trait he shared with his mother. Sorry I'm late.

Not an answer to my question, said Mr. Eliot.

Out, Arthur said. I was out and I didn't realize the time. I do apologize.

Rude to Rosie as well, said Mr. Eliot, who was finding this dinner something of a dark cloud.

Arthur spread his napkin. As far as Rosie was concerned, Arthur could do no wrong.

Your Gilbert Finch ought to give some thought to his future, Mr. Eliot said, not looking at his daughter. You may not think it's important, but it is.

We'll all be interested to see what happens, said Mrs. Eliot, flushed and happy.

Yes, we will, said Lilian with what she meant to be defiance. Her being with Gilbert Finch was a grand opening up of the world, a world that stretched far and away from this dining room table.

Just then Lilian looked down at her hand and saw with terror that the engagement ring she'd picked out with Gilbert at Mr. Parson's wasn't there. She excused herself from the table, ransacked her room, going through her pockets, looking under the bed. She paused for a moment before becoming hysterical. She sent off a note to the Somerset Club where she'd lunched, and one to the shop on Boylston Street where she'd gotten the towels, and finally one to the Searses' where she and Marian had been for tea. She hardly slept the night. In the morning she heard from Louis Joseph that they'd found nothing, and a withering note came from Elsie Sears saying they'd looked between the cushions of every chair but had turned up nothing. The phone rang. It was the Somerset Club. The ring had been found near the washbasins in the ladies' lounge.

Gilbert fetched it on his way to dinner that night, and put it once again on Lilian's finger. He appeared unruffled by the incident.

Have you done something to it? she said, gazing at him as if he were a magician. It seems to have gotten bigger.

Gilbert Finch merely shrugged.

I N EVERY direction lay the ocean as round as a saucer rimmed at the horizon where it met the sky. She sat on the ocean liner, taking her morning tea in the shade of a green awning with a writing tablet propped in her lap. On her left hand, holding down the fluttering paper, her ring sent off tiny sparks. *July 1, 1926,* she wrote. *My Dearest Love.*

Lilian Eliot was generally plunged in gloom having to be on a boat for an ocean crossing, and got the urge to jump off if they didn't land soon, but this time she was willing to sit on deck for hours and watch the horizon and the sea change color. She thought of Gilbert Finch, and of the way he signed his letters, Yrs, GPF. She would soon stop that.

She tried gin for the first time and her head spun — not the room merely her head. The son of a duke sat beside the Eliots on deck, but since he did nothing about it neither did they.

They arrived in Calais where the wind by the docks smelled of soaked wood and coffee. The first few hours traveling by train to Paris Lilian could not help think of her old friend, Walter Vail. She had pictured him here so often. So these were the yellow stripes of field he might have looked at, and these the dining car menus he was used to reading. She thought of him not with the old deep feeling but more mildly, in a sort of daydream. As one often feels in a foreign place, she half-expected to meet him at any moment — perhaps he was even on the train! Though he was revisiting her thoughts, he had long ago ceased to have any influence over her. So what if she did meet him? She would greet him warmly, in a way which would show him he'd long since been out of her mind. He, too, would act as if they'd meant nothing to each other, that nothing had taken place between them. Of course, on his side it was true. She had come to accept that. Perhaps his wife would be with him — yes, coming up from behind with a smart coat on and a stole. Darling, he would say, Véronique . . . and the brim of her hat would touch his shoulder. Lilian would shake the slip of a pale kid glove, look directly into her almond-shaped eyes. So nice to meet you, she'd say. Was she well? Walter Vail would be polite, his posture stiffened awkwardly. Never better, she would say and tell him of her engagement. Why that was wonderful news, congratulations. No he didn't think he'd met Gilbert Finch . . . Now her mother would be calling her — they were at the train station, people walking crisply by, and they would both have to hurry off . . . And after, Lilian couldn't help wishing him the tiniest bit of trouble, after what she'd been through on his account. Afterwards, his wife would press him about her — who was this girl from Boston? How good *une amie?* They would quarrel! Lilian meanwhile would leave the meeting serene, having seen his face, and seen that it was not the face she loved, not anymore.

Her heart beat faster, envisioning the scene. As she watched the wet ditches fly past below she found herself recalling some of the old hurt, and how unlike Gilbert he was, Gilbert whose face was so open that when an emotion appeared on it there was no chance of mistaking it for something else. Lilian thought of his face, savoring those qualities, yet seeing her own reflection over the countryside, she found it difficult to picture exactly.

In Paris, they stayed next door to where Empress Joséphine had lived. She had walked in the same park and Arthur reported that she'd changed her clothes three times a day, though Mrs. Eliot remained unimpressed.

They went to Versailles. Lilian saw Nancy Cobb sitting on a bench, and felt it couldn't possibly be she, then they both decided they knew each other and said hello. Nancy Cobb had heard about Lilian's engagement, and said she'd had a crush on Gilbert Finch long ago, but that he'd never liked her back. Remembering Benjy Rogers and how Nancy Cobb had eclipsed her so many summers before, Lilian was proud of Gilbert and found herself liking Nancy Cobb more because of it. Her parents had always wanted her to marry a doctor, Nancy said, and she guessed she'd never get the chance. A doctor? Lilian said. Nancy Cobb had an encouraging look. Oh, you must be thinking of Winn, Lilian said. Yes, that's right! Nancy Cobb said. I knew Gilbert wasn't the right name — it was Winn Finch. His brother, Lilian said. Oh, said Nancy Cobb, I guess I don't know Gilbert.

One rainy afternoon Lilian stayed a long time at the l'Orangerie, hushed by the Cézannes. Walking back through the Tuileries she saw the couples sharing umbrellas, and missed Gilbert more than ever, aching to feel his arm against hers.

She bought herself a present — the fatal effect of Paris — in the shape of a Persian miniature. Her father scorned it, thinking it decadent taste. Lilian found it prettier in opposition. It was of a forest with lots of snakes, and birds, and animals, with a man in pink riding through on a white horse. She put it against the foot of her bed to admire while she waited for breakfast.

The boulevards were teeming.

Everyone else dined at nine, but the latest the Eliots could stand was eight, staying a few minutes at the end to stare at the people. The ladies were dressed like Indians on the warpath.

A woman from Boston named Edith Quincy was in Paris, and Lilian had tea with her. She was quite changed from the last time Lilian had seen her when she'd come to help them farm on the shore in June. While weeding, Edith Quincy had told some rough stories which had made even Arthur pale, but now she was talking about what churches they ought to see and wanting to know the news from Boston. Lilian was sadly disappointed.

They went to dine in the Bois several times and drove around afterwards past the lake. The boats were out, each with a red Japanese lantern on it, carefully arranged to shed no light whatsoever on the interior. Lilian saw the shine of a woman's bracelet, the white of a man's collar deep in the shadows among the pooling red reflections. Later, back in her room with the night glow of Paris coming through the part in the curtains, she had difficulty getting to sleep.

Everything seemed to vibrate with expectation, and she was filled with a new spirit. She bought a new fur coat and chose a string of pearls. Mr. Eliot said her character was sadly changing. The next day she bought flowers for her hat and changed it further. Aunt Tizzy, who had joined them in Paris, gave her some towels for her trousseau: they were so thick with embroidery there was no place to dry your face. Lilian was delighted by such beautiful, useless things.

THEY MOTORED through Brittany and Burgundy visiting churches. Lilian preferred the small ones which
looked like barns and seemed twice as old as the Roman
ruins. She was not as fond of the grander churches which
Arthur liked, strolling through them with an authoritative
air, his heels clicking smartly on the stone, not intimidated
in the least by the vaulted ceilings and the cracked gaze of
the saints. In each church she would imagine herself walking down the aisle, with Gilbert standing at the end, then
her attention would be taken up by the marble drapes, or a
tiny altar painting of a woman in bed, and wedding visions
would disappear in a different sort of contemplation. When
she snapped out of it, she experienced an odd discomfort at
having forgotten her darling Gilbert for even a moment.

She wrote him letters. She wished they could go off and
live in a tent in the desert, but then decided she liked seeing
him with the other boys because he looked the nicest of all.
She read his letters over and wished for the kiss at the end.
Of course she had looked at the moon! She could not find
the words to tell him how much she loved him, but would
spend all her life trying to show him. She felt she might as
well have been dead before.

For a long time she couldn't read — the whole boat ride

over, if it wasn't about a couple she wasn't interested, and if it was she would think about the two of them and cease reading altogether. But after a while her brain came back to her and when she read she found she understood the books better than ever.

In Milan, they went to the zoo and Lilian grew spellbound watching a lion pace back and forth in its cage, the low eyes glancing at her lazily. She knew she ought to feel sorry for it, but the creature seemed so certain and secretive and wild she felt it ought to feel sorry for her.

She felt more in common with animals and dead artists — they'd been to the room by the Spanish Steps in Rome where Keats died — than with her family and the business of travel. Her mother fussed over increasing numbers of hatboxes and trunks, and her father, energetic all day, nodded off during after-dinner coffee. In Rome she was the only one with enough sand to stay up late, balcony doors open, waiting to hear a nightingale. Arthur was disappearing at intervals.

In Paris he had taken long excursions alone, sometimes coming in after dinner. I got completely lost, he'd say, which Mr. Eliot believed, finding no logic in the layout of European cities, but which Lilian, knowing him better, did not. Once she saw him shake confetti out of his hat brim. Now in Rome he would absent himself from lunch at a café and appear across the piazza — Mr. and Mrs. Eliot were not noticing — sharing a cigarette with a mustached fellow he seemed to know. Then there were the two women in fishnet stockings who drifted away from him when Lilian called from the top of the steps near the Borghese Gardens.

* * *

Look what we spend to feed her, said Mrs. Eliot with her back to the wide view of blue hills rising up from Lago di Como. And the horrid little thing gets no fatter. They were on the last leg of their trip in the northern lakes.

Lilian smiled lamely.

People eat too much, said Mr. Eliot. We could all live just as happily on bread and water. Before him on the table was a bowl of brown wheat.

Not me, said Arthur. He behaved as if he were accidentally placed with these people for breakfast.

Mrs. Eliot was watching with interest the other guests of the hotel. Well, our little jewel is not eating enough. She'll be a little wisp of a thing when she gets back to Mr. Finch.

Lilian smiled at the mention of Gilbert's name.

I've a wonderful five-mile walk today, Mr. Eliot said, and pressed a folded map near his plate.

Your wedding dress will be swimming on you, said Mrs. Eliot, but she was finding something interesting in the new arrivals. There's that little French man with the peculiar habits, she said. Lilian turned to see a man with a young woman on either arm.

They are most likely his daughters, said Mr. Eliot, frowning at his wife. Margaret, he warned.

Arthur observed them through his drooping lids. Stop staring, said Mrs. Eliot. Arthur ignored her.

It goes around the lake and there's a little place where they'll give you lunch, Mr. Eliot said.

I'd like to shoot, Arthur said.

I think we can manage that.

I have a church I want to see, Mrs. Eliot said.

Here? Lilian said. Her mother did not answer.

You have your choice, Lilian, said her father. Path or parish.

Neither! she wanted to scream. She missed Gilbert so much she could have burst. Everything here was so different, moving her in new and different ways, she wanted to wait for Gilbert, and to see it with him. It was as if she were holding part of herself back, saving it for when he'd be there with her. She felt that he would ground her, and through him she would *really* know things. She was not thinking how one sees things for the first time only once.

I'd like to see the hills, she said finally, wanting the exercise. It might help her sleep at night. She'd become so restless she wondered if she'd ever have a tranquil night's sleep again.

On their way back, they stopped in Paris one last time, and enlisted a Monsieur Troyat who had done the Sedgwicks' portraits to do theirs. Except that Mr. Eliot did not have time to sit — he was in Europe — and if he did need his portrait done, which he didn't think, he could just as well have it executed in Boston. Mrs. Eliot had overbooked herself for fittings, and anyway preferred to let stand the portrait of her done at twenty, and Arthur said he wouldn't be drawn until he was completely bald which he seemed to feel would not be in too long a time. Lilian was the only one to go for a sketch.

Monsieur Troyat sat her on a couch and gave her a diaphanous shawl to put over her shoulders. She watched his face as he drew, a tidy man with a pince-nez clipped to his nose and a beard. They spoke a bit about her getting married.

He is a nice boy? said Monsieur Troyat.

Oui, yes. *Très gentil.*

And do the tips of your fingers and the ends of your hairs tingle when you see him? He spoke like a strict instructor, emphatically, his hand always moving across his paper.

Lilian smiled politely.

Because there must be passion, he went on.

Lilian continued to look at the stuffed parrot he had ordered her to gaze at.

Very important for the passion, he said, nodding.

Lilian thought of her experience with passion, the sort that Monsieur Troyat was talking about, and knew that it was not as appealing as it sounded. She found her feelings for Gilbert Finch, and the certainty of him, to be far more satisfying, a better passion. Yes, she said.

For the man I mean, he said and looked at her with intensity, stopped in his sketching. To love a woman in whom I did not inspire passion would be an unbearable thing. He added quickly as he went back to the paper, I'd think.

The likeness of the finished portrait was good. Lilian's dark eyes were as warm on the paper as in life, though her brow shadowed them more in the drawing, her hair had its fuzzy, loose halo. But she was disturbed to see how her hands had been rendered — only a few strokes, but they suggested something disturbing — one pressed to her rib in a defensive way, the other clutching her skirt.

I call this, said Monsieur Troyat in his monotone, the Bride-to-Be.

THEY'D COME to Scotland for their honeymoon. Being early in October the days were growing shorter and the evening air had an extra chill to it which Lilian found delicious. In the mornings the glass between the lead panes was dewed over and the countryside behind a green and brown blur. From where they sat in the breakfast room of the hotel, they could see the trees and bushes in the morning sunlight. Rain left large drops on the branches and they sparkled pink and yellow. Lilian remarked how the whole world had turned charming on their account.

The wedding had happened in a trance, the bridesmaids in blue with darker blue velvet hats, Lilian in the simplicity of satin. Gilbert stood soft-shouldered at the end of the altar — the moment she'd entered King's Chapel was frozen in her mind — and when she saw him she thought, He will always be in my life. The girls were all arrayed — Jane's stick-thin arms poking out of the blue velvet sleeves, Dolly turned back to look at the guests, her dark head in two shiny parts, her eyes vivid. Irene smiled wanly, her lost face floating above the long neck. Marian rearranged the chrysanthemums in her bouquet to her satisfaction, and Sis stood at the end, in wobbly shoes. Down next to Gilbert was his brother Winn who, having been through this already, felt himself an old hand. She could see the back of her mother's head, the twisted coil of hair beneath her hat, the dangling pearls, then when she turned her face, her mother's expression of having stumbled in upon this scene and finding it lovely. In the pew behind was Hildy in a simple hat, her head bowed as if the grand spectacle were too much to bear. Across the aisle was the solitary round figure of Dr. Finch, hands clasped to the small of his back, chin lifted, waiting for the ceremony to commence and be over. He had little tolerance for social events.

Lilian walked down the aisle beside Mr. Eliot, his hawk profile glimpsed out of the corner of her eye, the flag of his white hair, his face smooth and lean, the candlelight bending in his glasses. She walked in a dream, her arm around his, feeling the material of his suit under her hand, and it occurred to her she'd never taken his arm this way before.

The ceremony was a blur.

Afterwards they danced on the stones in the back garden of the Somerset Club. Gilbert placed his palm on her back and took small steps, smiling with his lips closed. Jane sat against some latticework with Jack Ives, neither of them being one for dancing. Dolly tried to get the band to play something jazzy, but their efforts surpassed their skill, momentarily clearing the dance floor. Bobby Putnam seemed not to notice that Arthur was hogging Irene Putnam, and Aunt Tizzy had a splendid time chatting with Emmett Smith, discussing their mutual pals. Madelaine Fenwick was there looking very French, having just been to Paris, and Lilian felt wonderfully jaded that she did not think of Walter Vail till afterwards. It was not such a bad thing to have a past, she thought, especially if one ended with happiness.

In Scotland they took long walks over the hills, stopping on the little rises. Lilian folded some heather into a hand-kerchief for a keepsake. They visited castles with reflecting ponds and stood in open doorways of crumbling stone ruins out in the middle of drizzling moors.

One evening they were driving back to the hotel over narrow roads and bridges. The sun was down, the sky as deep blue as the glass goblets at the Ritz, and Lilian watched the scenery floating by the open window. She caught glimpses of the bay, then a bank of trees — gnarled bark, floppy leaves — then stone walls, then the bay again. She rested her head against Gilbert's shoulder and looked up at the leaves darkening. It had not been such a long time ago she'd been alone looking at things, and she could re-member as a distant glimmer the keenness of feeling she might have had, seeing the vista of the sea or a patch of morning light on a corner of grass, or stepping out of a back door in the night, and it occurred to her that the feeling now in the car may have been happier, but it was also more dull. Gilbert's presence beside her, his cigar-scented wool jacket, his soft fingers, kept out the harshness of the world and of her feeling shaky in it. When his hand rested on her back in an unthinking way as they stepped up a tumbled path of rocks, she felt transformed, connected back to herself. What softness she felt! And added to that was the fact that everything, herself and the things around her, felt soft, too, and blurred.

But the softness was easy to like. It was a veil obscuring things. It must have been what opium was like, she de-cided. Had she been alone, the scene before her might have seized ahold of her heart, but since she'd shared a bed with this man — the dark nights rustling — she felt drugged, unmoved by the old things. How would that thatched roof have looked to her before? Would the stretching bay have echoed something stretching in her? She made a vague effort to imagine it but found that, nestled against Gilbert Finch's shoulder, silent beneath the car's motor, she did not care in the least to find out.

On one of their last mornings, very early, before anyone stirred out in the halls or beneath them, Lilian was awakened by a loud downpour. The rain pounded the wide terrace off their room. The stone wall was swathed in shivering ivy. Lilian got up and stood at the terrace doors, the water was rattling down. Out on the bay she could see hooded fishermen bent over their lines. She opened the door and the sound of rain was louder in the room, waking Gilbert. He came and stood beside her. Her heart quickened. She put her arm out, out of the stuffy air of the room, and immediately the light fabric of her nightgown was soaked through, thrilling her. She took Gilbert's hand, pulling at him to step outside. There was a glint in her eye which had only recently appeared, surprising from this quiet girl from Boston.

Now now, he said, pulling back. We'd get soaked.

Lilian nodded, with the new bright look.

Gilbert shook his head and smiled. Come on, he said, and the protective arm came around her, and he placed a guiding hand on the small of her back. It felt oddly prohibitive. Back to bed. He spoke gently, as always, with encouragement, and she went with him, docile, yielding, but with the faint disturbed sense that she'd discovered how it felt to be, for a moment, otherwise.

IV

Gilbert Finch

THE WEDDING presents had been brought to the house on Joy Street. The large gilt mirror from Aunt Tizzy was up in the hall, Uncle Nat and Aunt Peg's silver George II coffeepot in the dining room. There was an Italian leather portfolio edged in gold from Irene Putnam, a beautiful tablecloth with lace holes in it from Jack and Jane, and from Dolly and Freddie Vernon a studded leather bellows. Mr. and Mrs. Eliot gave them the sideboard they'd promised Lilian, and Gilbert's father contributed to the dining room with eight ribbon-backed Chippendale chairs, circa 1770. From Winn Finch and his wife, Edith, four volumes of Goldsmith with colored plates. Marian and Dickie Wiggin were extravagant with a set of yellow teacups decorated with birds. Sis and Cap Sedgwick donated a simple silver tray. Hildy made her gift herself, a bureau duster embroidered with butterflies on each end, and Arthur bought them an elaborate picnic basket, with plaid flasks and leather straps, the sort of thing one always means to but never does use.

When she returned from Scotland to the new house Lilian felt herself a new person. She was Mrs. Gilbert P. Finch. The trip had been like being in the clouds, and in coming back, she had to stop floating. Still, she'd been changed by the flight, and everything looked different.

She tried to hold on to the airy feeling. In the mornings with the dew wet on the wrought-iron spikes by the doorways, and filled with a new energy, she walked down Beacon Hill and across the street to the Public Garden. She went along the meandering path, past clipped flower beds and statues — men on horseback, soldiers — around the pond dotted with ducks. The swan boats with their winged sides were shut away for the winter. At the southern gates, she saw the uniformed porters blowing whistles outside the Ritz. The last time she'd been there was for Sis Sedgwick's wedding one chilly day in April, before she'd known Gilbert really, and she felt less in common with the girl she'd been then than with the strangers she watched in foreign coats and bright makeup ducking into cars beneath the hotel awning. She moved briskly along her route, crossing the street to the Common where the grass was less tended; there were more people here, and the trees towered above the esplanade. Through the leaves she could see the dome of the State House with its pounded gold surface. She thought idly of Emerson and the feeling of perpetual youth he'd experienced crossing the Common at twilight with the snow puddles. But mostly her mind was empty of the usual things — that is, she thought of Gilbert. She thought of how they were married. She could think of that in various ways for a long time. She thought of his briefcase snapping closed in the morning when he headed off for work on Milk Street. She thought of his coat bunched at his shoulders. She pictured his ties hanging on the tie rack in their room and thought of their bed, and of how he would sometimes turn to her at night and sometimes not, and thinking this way she would find herself back on Joy Street without having noticed where she'd walked.

But Boston was not so changed and the old things trickled back in with peculiar effect.

She had lunch with Dolly Vernon and Marian Wiggin, both old married ladies as they saw it. They pored over the same topics, other people, who was engaged, who had cut whom, how the children were behaving. Dolly talked about Freddie's family and described a ball she'd been to with an insect theme. Marian had gone to dinner at the Amorys' and said it was frightfully grand. Dolly wondered if she should cut her hair the way other girls were doing — Sis Sedgwick had cut hers which was daring for Sis — and Marian said she didn't think she herself had the nerve. Lilian had promised Gilbert never to cut off her hair and remained silent. In the powder room, she thought that her being married had changed her more than she realized. She felt as if she were filled up completely with Gilbert Finch and had nothing else to say to anyone.

Of course there was the house to occupy her. She'd had a new banister put in and the pipes replaced in the kitchen. The dining room chairs were upholstered in a reasonable French silk, new curtains were measured for the guest rooms. She felt she was spinning a cocoon.

She read, but that was different too. The people in her books — for she thought of them as people rather than characters — were no longer the dazzling spirits near to her face the way they'd once been, sending off waves of sensation, now they were more like companions, sitting across the room in armchairs, the way her dearest Gilbert did, at night home from the office.

Everything was shifted.

One Friday afternoon in February Gilbert came home early from work, surprising Lilian. It was an Indian summer day, and since they'd not put out the iron garden furniture, Lilian had carried out a rush-seated chair from inside and was sitting with her back to the bricks and shriveled ivy, facing the tiny plot of land they expansively called the garden, reading a book in the thin sunshine.

When he stepped out of the french doors Lilian jumped a little, and he put both hands on her arm to calm her, smiling, hiding his teeth as if to contain his happiness. She smiled back. His coat was rumpled and his tie was off to the side. At first she didn't understand his liquid slow manner. It was the weather, she thought, which made it seem as if they were underwater. He took her elbow, and pulled her to her feet in one languid motion. Then she understood.

Lilian would always remember how from their room they could hear Maureen moving pots in the kitchen, and could hear a motorcar backfire down in the street.

One night she was upstairs when Gilbert came in, and after she finished her letter came down and found him in the living room in a chair by the bay window, staring into space. She asked him if anything were wrong. The way the fading light caught the shadows made his face look as if it were collapsing. He frowned, not turning in her direction, and said no, with a sort of scorn she'd never heard from him, except after a few cocktails, but never aimed at her. She was miserable that night, mentioned nothing about it at dinner, and lying in bed thought of Aunt Tizzy's talk about marriage having its difficult moments and realized this was one. It was as if she did not know Gilbert anymore.

There was nothing to do. In her family it was never done to talk to a man in a mood. Her mother had always gone wisely silent when Mr. Eliot went under a dark cloud, and glided over to the bar and occupied herself with a drink until the mood passed. Unfortunately for Lilian, she did not like the taste of alcohol and was left to suffice with feeling.

The next night it was raining and Lilian hovered near the front door to be there when Gilbert got home. When she helped him off with his coat he looked at her anxiously, smiling in his old way. She felt their old rapport. The short estrangement made their coming together all the sweeter. But Lilian did not forget his dark cloud, and wondered when it would descend on him again.

LILIAN AND GILBERT had help. They were never alone in the house on Joy Street.

Maureen Conner, in the kitchen, was good at stews and pies. She'd come over from County Kerry and lived in one of the narrow maid's rooms on the third floor. Maureen had a pudding face and fat neck, small eyes, and teeth which slanted back into her mouth like a rodent's. Peeling apples, she always looked disappointed, as if the fruit didn't measure up to her ideal. Maureen shook her head at the ways of the world, older than her twenty-eight years. In the mornings Lilian had seen her slip out of the house into the Beacon Hill fog to catch the 6 A.M. mass, a lace mantilla draped over her head. In her room there was a standing crucifix and wooden rosary beads pooled on her bedside table.

Anna lived in the next room on the third floor. She'd done housework since she was fourteen. While Maureen washed dishes, Anna would sit at the table with a cigarette; her teeth were badly stained by tobacco, but otherwise she was crisp and clean. When she dusted she squared things off, making block arrangements on Lilian's dresser which Lilian didn't like but didn't ask her to change. Lilian simply moved them out into a looser placement herself. Kate came in four days a week from the South End to do the laundry, occasionally with a black eye.

One gardener was dismissed after Kate complained of his being too familiar, and was replaced by Rod, who neglected the little plot of grass in the back in favor of the flower beds. Lilian caught his enthusiasm for bulbs and blossoms and had a greenhouse built off the back where Rod shuffled around in untied shoes. They had chives in the winter and the smell of geraniums when it snowed.

A man with owllike eyebrows named Louis drove for them, and when he could not, his brother, also called Louis, filled in.

Lilian had grown up with servants, and assumed her own household would run as smoothly as her mother's, but it was not so automatic. She had to repeat instructions a number of times, how Mr. Finch liked his steak cooked, where Rod should coil and leave the hose, how pleats would keep if ironed on both sides. Now and then, hearing herself in the role, she would wonder how much it mattered really, bothering with such small things, and, exasperated, would go out for a walk or shut herself in the library to read a diary of escape from the French Revolution. There would always be a knock at the door — Kate wanting to know where to put the new chair some men had brought — and she'd be reeled back into the business of running the house. It was, after all, what she was there to do.

Then the children came. Lilian was shocked to discover what a messy business childbirth was — no one had told her — and afterwards she joined the secret club and didn't talk about it either. First came Fay, who shrieked, then Sally who didn't. Gilbert was pleased with his girls. He jiggled their little hands and patted their little beribboned heads. Gilbert still got into his moods now and then, but Lilian was used to them; with the children she noticed them less and less, and the worry was less as well.

Their third child was a son, Porter, and Gilbert rewarded Lilian with a string of pearls. They decided to do their best not to have any more, three was enough. So on certain evenings where before they might have lain flushed beside one another, they were now satisfied with a light kiss and holding hands for a while.

Fay had been christened at three months and Lilian saved the flowers from around the christening bowl, and pressed them in the Bible, but they did not get around to baptizing Sally or Porter. Why, Lilian could not have said; she went to church on holidays, but church was not large in their lives.

As a little girl, Fay climbed into strangers' laps, and pointed to a mole and said they had some dirt on them. She was a shiny child with dark glistening hair and eyes like compasses. Sally was fat and white, with Gilbert's heavy mouth and Lilian's block chin. She followed Fay around and was told by Fay what to do. Porter, from birth, had a forehead which knuckled and penetrating eyes which did not look away when meeting people for the first time.

It changed things of course when the children came, but they had planned on that. Gilbert, with his shirtsleeves rolled up, rode the girls around on his shoulders, grinning, handing them off to Lilian with a frightened look when they began to cry. Lilian would calm them and hand them off to Anna, who was firm with them, squaring them off on their little routines, just as she had done with the furniture.

H E WORKED with men named Mr. Frye and Mr. Winter and Mr. Baldwin. There was also Joe Morgan,
Bill O'Brien and Ken Stone. Gilbert didn't talk much
about the actual work, but he did mention these people.
Also, the typists Mrs. Templeton and Miss Lyne, their
names came up too. Part of Gilbert's job entailed traveling
to New Haven and New London, and occasionally Providence, and when he returned would tell Lilian if the trips
had gone well, or that the leaves were changing in New
Bedford a little later than in Boston, or that in Providence
it was always raining. Sometimes he went to the docks to
meet shipments, but mostly he was hovering over figures
at his desk and having meetings. He wasn't particularly
attached to his job at White, Frye & Co., Lilian knew that,
but one did need to have work.

After he'd been there four years he stopped talking about
Mr. Frye in the front office, or mentioning Ken Stone's
flirtation with Miss Lyne, and Lilian wondered if he might
be thinking about leaving. Before they were married, he
had told her that he wanted to do something different,
eventually, possibly something in the civic sphere. Now, he
found it was time to consider it more seriously.

Lilian watched him as she had watched him play curling

in the first years they were married, arching forward and holding his position while he watched how far the stone got, though now she watched him through the narrow hall windows move slowly up and down the front steps. She would feel relieved or worried, depending on Gilbert's mood, and felt this was a sign of her love. Since he was a man, with the freedom to act, she watched to see what choices he would make, since his choices would determine her life. Not only did she not think of making certain choices herself, she was completely unaware of having the desire to do so.

Lilian assumed that the reason Gilbert had seemed more troubled lately had to do with his job, that he was thinking of leaving it. Sometimes, before his glass of Scotch, she noticed an ashen color across his cheeks. When they went out to dine he would give Lilian the signal to leave — a finger across his throat — before dessert was even served.

It was 1929 and their friends were prospering. The Iveses had just bought a new yacht and were spending the summer on it. The Vernons had moved into a larger house and the Wiggins were putting a greenhouse on their place in Beverly Farms.

Usually Lilian made sure to see one of her lady friends for a morning visit or tea, something away from the house and children, but one day she noticed as she got ready for bed that she'd not found the time. It occurred to her that she'd not made time the day before either.

The next day, while the children were napping, Lilian went to the sewing room to get a lamp which needed repairing and heard Anna and Maureen down at their end of the hall chatting and laughing girlishly. When her footsteps on the bare threshold reached them, they stopped. Lilian felt oddly uncomfortable in her own house.

As she sat in the drawing room while the children were being bathed it seemed as if she had not exchanged an interesting word with anyone all day. Into this stillness Gilbert came home. She perched forward on the edge of her chair showing him a bright look, ripe for conversation. She tried to think of what she had to say for herself, and watched as he placed his briefcase against the desk leg where he always placed it. His jacket sleeve had caught at the elbow and was hooked high on his arm. She knew Gilbert would not be interested that she'd laid new paper on the linen closet shelves, wouldn't care about her having found the andirons for the library. Reading the other night about the American Revolution, she'd learned that Tommy Lattimore's great-great-great-something or other had been at Concord Bridge. She mentioned this to Gilbert. His eyebrows rose ever so slightly and his head nodded gently, but there was no further conversation. How had his day been? He was at the bar, pouring a drink. He shrugged, clinking the ice cubes in his glass. Business as usual, he said.

Gilbert did not care for talk. As far as he could see, most people in the world talked too much already and he would rather not add to the din. At dinner parties Gilbert could sit through a whole course without exchanging a word with his dinner partner, not out of fury or disgust, but because he was the sort of man who couldn't imagine that a person would rather chatter about nothing than silently enjoy eating his food. This attitude was in Boston perfectly acceptable. In addition, Gilbert was incapable of talking on the phone.

The children came down to say goodnight and Gilbert called Fay Sally, perplexing the girls. Fathers didn't mix up names. At dinner Lilian gently inquired if there were something on his mind.

No, he said. The annoyed tone had come back.

They were eating pork and string beans and nice mashed potatoes which Maureen made creamy. The odd idea occurred to Lilian that were Maureen to stand behind the swinging door to the pantry, she would hear no conversation whatsoever coming from the dining room. Lilian had learned to sit silently through these moods of Gilbert's, but on this particular day she found it difficult to do so. She thought of her parents and how they'd sat in silence too, but instead of making her feel more at home, it irritated her further.

Lilian regarded her husband's form, slumped forward on the table. Hard day? she said.

Gilbert turned his pleading eyes to her. He set down his silverware as if it had grown unwieldy — he could no longer manage it. Lily, I feel crummy. Would you mind if I skipped dessert and went and lay down?

Dear, of course not. She stood up.

No, he said. You stay. Finish.

He left the room and she heard his footsteps thudding lethargically up the carpeted stair. She tried to listen for the sound of him entering their room, and after sitting unhappily for a few moments, realized he must have already gone in, she was just too far away to hear.

* * *

At five o'clock in the morning she found him sitting on the small needlepoint stool in the library, staring into the empty black fireplace. The sky was still dark, though the light between the lilac leaves was turning a dim blue against the window.

Gilbert? She crossed her arms over her nightdress. She'd not put on a robe or slippers. What is it? She spoke in a patient tone.

Gilbert Finch shook his head. She could barely make out his profile, his bottom lip heavy and round. After some moments he said, I'm not sure I could say. The lip tightened. Not sure I know.

He looked to her like a creature at the bottom of the sea growing on a rock, a silent creature whose ecological purpose had run out. He sat hunched on the stool, his palms curled on his knees, his knees nearly level with his shoulders. She was becoming used to the silhouette, the slouch of no hope. It suddenly flashed on her — maybe he would not learn how to adapt. The adaptation which needed to be done wasn't easy, but one made the effort. She was doing it, wasn't she?

She tried to keep impatience out of her voice. Will you be coming back to bed? She understood how he felt. She, too, would have liked to throw up her hands sometimes, but she had been taught not to give up. One just made do.

Where else? he said, and the face he turned toward her was one she hardly knew.

On the way up the stairs she wondered if perhaps he wasn't being the more brave one after all.

ARTHUR ELIOT liked to argue, and was quick to con-
tradict people at the earliest opportunity. He had long
since given up trying to do this with Lilian who merely
ignored him and laughed. Mr. Eliot, however, remained
susceptible and displayed a special brand of irritability
when his son was near. But Arthur had not been around
much these days.

Mr. and Mrs. Eliot had sold the house on Fairfield Street
and made the expected move to Brookline, where they lived
just down Curtis Road from the other Eliots, Nat and Peg.
The sizable brick house had white pillars around a crescent
doorstep, a gravel driveway, and a wall of pine trees which
prevented them from seeing, or being seen, by the other
large houses nearby. Arthur didn't like the remoteness of
Curtis Road. He had been searching for places to write, and
over the years had wound up in resorts — the South of
France in the spring, Newport in the summer, the Alps in
the winter, places not especially conducive to writing, but
colorful. Having some money, he could afford this life,
meanwhile satisfying a demand by hostesses in need of a
single man.

Lilian saw him on his visits home after he'd stopped at
Brookline, slept, eaten Rosie's food, and irritated his father

before setting out again to broaden his horizons, always important for a writer to do. He came to see Lilian on Joy Street.

It is tiresome, Arthur said, how all Bostonians think they're superior to the rest of the world. He lay languidly back against the sofa, having helped himself to a gin at the bar. He was looking thinner than ever, his cheekbones giving him the look of a skull.

I'm afraid, Lilian said, they wouldn't lower themselves for a comparison.

Exactly, he said. So how do you stand it?

I don't know anything else, she said.

Arthur ran his fingers along a side table, not lifting his arm. This is nice, he said idly.

Mrs. Parish's, she said, from the auction.

Arthur nodded.

I do have Gilbert, she said simply. And the children.

I would hardly call Gilbert a saving grace. Arthur sat up. Much as I like the fellow. And anyone can have children.

Gilbert's a Bostonian and you like *him,* she said. Course he's not like the Wiggins or the Fenwicks, still, his family —

That reminds me, Arthur interrupted. I ran into your friend from the war.

Walter? There was a slight change in Lilian's face.

The one you were so keen on. Arthur lit a cigarette and spoke between locked teeth. I saw him in Monte Carlo — didn't I tell you? — I thought I did. Anyway, he's married to a French girl I guess. Rather rich she looked.

I did hear that.

Arthur watched the smoke blow away from him.

And? Lilian said.

That's all, just saw him. We had a drink. Arthur stood up and fingered a paperweight on the desk.

And how was he?

Fine, fine. Arthur tensed his rail shoulders. He frowned into the blue glass, considering another subject.

Have you been writing? she said.

This seemed to awaken him. Trying, trying, he said, and turned toward her with an intense look, as if she'd just reminded him what was important. I realized that all the stuff I'd been writing was hogwash, but now I'm onto something better, much better. I think it could be really good, if only —

I'd love to read something, Lilian said.

Arthur paced back and forth in front of her, shaking his head. His cigarette ash dropped to the floor. He glanced up, startled. I wouldn't dream of showing it, he said. God, not yet!

They say it takes a long time, Lilian said, feeling prim.

Yes, he said tightly. It does. He picked up his hat, the subject having become too distressing for him. Listen, I have to go —

You won't wait for Gilbert?

I would, but . . . Arthur sat down abruptly, close to Lilian on the sofa, his knees against her knees, his fingertips white on the hat brim. I need a loan, he said.

Lilian's gaze fell on him as it had many times before. Arthur, she said.

His head dropped. I know, he said. I know what you're

going to say. I'm irresponsible, I'm undependable. I know. Believe me, I know it better than anyone. His face hung like a dog's in front of her. It's only till my next quarter — I can't ask the Pater, you know that.

I know, she said. The way their money was given could not be changed. In a small voice she said, How much do you need?

He quoted a figure, aiming his gaze at the rug.

What?

Less would do.

That's nearly half Gilbert's annual salary, Lilian said.

But you don't live on his salary. Arthur turned his innocent face to her. Do you?

No, but . . . Lilian stood up, shaking a chill off her. Arthur looked after her, contrite, pleading. He shrugged as if to say, How much does money matter to us?

This really is the last time, she said with a firm expression. She sat down at the red Chinese desk, opened the leather book and frowned as she wrote out her brother's name.

O NE AFTERNOON Lilian spent hours with the Eliot genealogy books tracing back her connection to John Loring Moffat. Her father had given her some portrait copies, and on the back of one in tiny script she delineated with dates and middle names all the people who came between herself and John Loring Moffat. *Judge John Loring Moffat died at Barnstable 1799, 84 years old. His son Daniel Henry was made Solicitor General of Mass. He was first stationed in Portland, province of Maine. He came to Boston and lived at Somerset Street. He built a large house in Cambridge (this house where Radcliffe College was started) and died there November 15, 1853, aged 73 years. He married Henrietta Freeman, daughter of Constant Freeman, brother of James Freeman, minister at King's Chapel. They had thirteen children. Their oldest daughter Evelyn (Daisy) married William Arthur Eliot, 1783–1873 . . .*

She presented Gilbert with the little card when he returned late again from work, and he looked it over briefly.

I'm glad you're taking care of this business, Lily, he said. On his way up the stairs, he said, You should show that to Winn. He likes that sort of thing.

They were having dinner that Friday night with the

other Finches. It was a bitter November evening, and Lilian brought her genealogical research with her.

Winn and Edith Finch lived in a wide bay-windowed house on Beacon Street two blocks from the Garden. Edith was a small woman with dry blinking eyes and a limp from contracting polio as a teenager. She wore a long wool dress with lacy edges and was always polite and gracious. She and Winn had met in New York where she was getting a master's degree in architectural preservation and Winn was doing his residency at Columbia Presbyterian. It had at first surprised Lilian that Winn Finch had chosen a woman like Edith after having been involved with the more intriguing Irene Minter, but now she saw how they suited each other. Winn was a serious, conscientious person and his wife shared this attitude. Winn was larger than Gilbert, and more forceful, with a loud voice and strapping shoulders. He looked especially imposing beside the trim, limping figure of his wife, a contrast neither of them seemed to notice.

Before dinner they sat in the library with their drinks. Gilbert had two Scotches in fifteen minutes. He had been sick with the flu and looked more rumpled than usual. Being a doctor, Winn took a professional tone and inquired about his health. He regarded Gilbert solemnly.

Nothing to it, Gilbert said, as if rumors had been circulating about his health.

Lilian showed Winn Finch her research and he picked out that Louisa Moffat was a cousin of Edith's by marriage.

Winn went to the bookshelf and pulled out the Finch genealogy — Which you have of course, he said to Lilian

— and showed her where an Eliot ancestor had married a Finch.

They didn't have any children, Winn said.

Lilian noticed in the tiered configurations on the page that there were many people who did not marry.

Died young, Winn said. Or the Finch madness.

Lilian looked alarmed.

Oh, it's just what we call it, the eccentrics of the family, Winn said. His voice lowered. Though they have been known to shoot their wives. You won't find that in here, though. He tapped the book.

At dinner they talked about the crash. The Cunninghams were hardly touched since Mr. Cunningham didn't believe in investing. Cap Sedgwick had been hurt, but they still had the property in Milton and in Maine. Gilbert began talking about an ivy plant his secretary had let die, trying to illustrate, one assumed, that morale was down everywhere.

Edith blinked with interest. She offered more Newburgh to her guests.

It was so dark in the back of the house, Gilbert said. Everyone exchanged glances. He was drunk.

He began to tell again about the secretary's ivy plant, describing it word for word in the same way. His shoulders sloped in a crestfallen posture, and his eyes looked haunted. Even Winn with his robust spirit dared not interrupt him.

Edith tried to steer the conversation to another subject, asking about the children. Gilbert looked at her with an open, matter-of-fact gaze and said she was just like their mother. Except that Mother was more beautiful, he said. And amusing.

More than his silences, more than his evening irritations, it was this unkindness which made Lilian realize that Gilbert was sick. While Edith saw to the coffee tray and Winn answered a phone call from a patient, Lilian sat with Gilbert on the window seat.

Would you like to go home? she said in a cold voice, having lost sympathy with him after his attack on Edith. His eyes met hers, blank, then he hiccuped. He looked at his knee resting on the cushion, hiccuping again. It was only when she noticed his cheeks were wet that Lilian realized what the hiccuping was. By then it had quite taken him over.

THE DOCTOR advised a trip. He's worn himself out and needs a rest, he said. He knew of a splendid place in England.

Cap Sedgwick came to say good-bye. He shook Lilian's hand, tipping aside his long head so as not to meet her eye. Sis Sedgwick had said her good-byes earlier.

Do send him our love — if it seems wise to, said Cap Sedgwick, and he bowed away. There was a hushed aspect to the departure.

Sometimes the sun came out and gave a sharper curve to the hills rolling blandly off to the horizon, but mostly the light was wilted and pale. The children called the back yard the fairy garden for its resemblance to scenes in their storybooks, with the scattered snowdrops and crooked apple trees. The house, too, was like the illustrations: a thatched roof like a brimless hat, the dark beams imbedded in white stucco. Inside was a jumble of rooms, small hallways connected by steps, banisters flush to the wall. The windows had square lead panes and the ceilings were slanted. In the living room was lumpy furniture, and Lilian removed knickknacks from around the house in case they would be there for long. They stayed nineteen months.

By the time winter came, the rosebush around the gate was a tangle of thorns, and the ground could be muddy one day, hard as rock the next. Lilian walked every day through the little town with three pubs and not much else, along the high-banked roads, and over the fields. It was a mile and a half to the clinic and she would arrive with a glow in her cheeks, distinguishing her from the inhabitants of the building, who were pasty and overfed. She visited in the morning before lunch and often in the afternoons while the children rested, and looked forward to these walks as time alone.

Gilbert had a light by his bed and steam heat, both rare things in England as far as they had seen, so he counted himself lucky. The doctors came and pressed the glands at his jaw, looking off. Another sort of doctor came also, Dr. Howze, who stood at the foot of the bed with a great expanse of forehead and asked Gilbert questions. At the end of his inquiry, Dr. Howze asked him: Would you like to talk with me? and Gilbert replied that that's what he thought he had been doing for ten minutes. Dr. Howze nodded and squinted his eyes.

Separated from his wife and children, fed soft food, and made to nap, Gilbert retained a baffled air. If he took any comfort in being treated like a baby, he did not convey the notion to his wife. His face grew creamier and softer, with jowls appearing. Lilian was struck by the whiteness of him, even his eyes seemed more pale. Propped up with pillows, blending in with the bedclothes, if it weren't for the small bracelet on his wrist, Lilian thought, he would be the picture of contentment.

To his brother Winn he wrote:

I've discovered that the James Winthrops are descended from the Langtrys of Kent, not the William Langtrys but the Harold Langtrys. They have Bell Island in the Hebrides. I hope you are looking in on the lawn on Joy Street. It must be awfully dug up. Let me know if we should order some turf.

He wrote his father:

Dear Father,

I've not been able to see much of the countryside. I'm not sure what you'd think of the organization here but know you would find it different from Boston. There is a lot of talk. I find it difficult to read so they read aloud and it sounds like babbling fields. The children come to see me once a week and their faces rise like moons. Porter is a regular gentleman. If we don't get him back soon he'll have a Brit accent. Tell Ellie I got the socks and thank her. I hope if the weather is there it is braced. I am holding on to the shelf.

Your son,
Gilbert Finch

He wrote his nephew:

Dear Winthrop,

Your father sent me your card with the picture of the ship which I very much enjoyed and thank you for. They are making me as best they can here which in England means feeding me milk thirteen times a day. I have taught them how to make chocolate milkshakes so it's not so bad. I hope you have succeeded in getting Sparkie to sit. It's important to train a puppy early. One cannot underestimate the effect of early good habits. Your father would back me up on that.

> Fondly,
> Uncle Gilbert

But he also wrote to Winn:

There is something black in my heart which I don't dare mention except to tell you that it's there. I can't seem to beat it.

There was a pile of books on his little night table and, in the weeks since he'd arrived, he'd not touched one of them. Lilian read aloud when she visited. Sometimes Gilbert did not want to talk, and the doctors had told her that it was important to let him be, lest he become ashamed of his condition.

One afternoon, after they had been in England a few months, he asked her to come sit on the bed. He looked especially ragged and his upper lip was swollen more than usual, filled with emotion.

I'm sorry I'm putting you through this, he said in a weak voice.

I know that, Lilian said and patted his arm. It was difficult to look at him.

You must be sorry you married me, he said, and this time it was Gilbert's real voice, coming from the man deep inside.

Lilian felt a strong emotion run through her, feeling that

he had come back to her. And what would the children think of that? She smiled.

He took her hand gratefully, and she returned the pressure: here was Gilbert again, but after a moment, out of fatigue or lack of interest, he let it go.

For two days at Christmas time Gilbert was let out of the clinic to be with his family. He sat by the fire, dressed in clothes which had grown tight, wearing slippers, and made a supreme effort to appear involved in the family activities. The children called out to him to look at their presents, at what they were doing, but conscious of his infirmity, he used a tentative voice. Pa, they said, Pa. Maureen, who, with Anna, had come abroad with the Finches, made a plum pudding which Gilbert complimented her on, yet other than a vague comment about the branches taking over the windows, he hardly said a word.

In the bedroom which Lilian thought of as hers, since Gilbert had not seen it till now, there were two twin beds. Lilian helped Gilbert into the bed she slept in and sat on the edge of it as she had sat on his bed at the clinic — in fact, it felt quite the same. She had hoped to be close to him, but till now had kept the hope in the back of her mind, not wanting to be disappointed.

Night, my darling, she said and bent to kiss him.

He looked at her with pale, pitying eyes. Poor Lily, he said.

Not at all, she said and smiled for him. It took her a long while to fall asleep.

Dear Winn,

Everyone is feeling today the suicide of a woman here only two weeks ago. They don't tell us but of course we know. She used the cord which held down her mattress pad to hang herself. Any of us could have been there, knowing her feeling. One feels both sides of it, hers and ours, with the act having happened under our roof.

The children come once a week. Fay scowls and Sally stands with sagging lip. Porter marches off to investigate things. Sometimes it keeps off certain thoughts to see them till for no reason my mind blackens and I think they would be better off without me. I wouldn't say so to Lilian, she watches with enough worry. I marvel at her every day, I'm sure she doesn't know. Will you tell her?

I don't know how.

Edith's books are lovely. The nurses read them to me aloud. Please thank her.

Love,
Gilbert Finch

He wrote in other moods.

. . . It was the crazy things which spoke in me and I listened, you should too because they make sense, they speak the truth instead of plopping down words unthought like one does in the hallway. Think of all the idiocy coming out of people who say things because there they are, face to face, in the hall or with a pen or entertaining a room filled with people.

. . . Dr. Howze tries to get me to write though I don't always seem to make sense I know, the idea being that to drain the poison out or something along those lines will lessen the power of it. I'm not sure the brain drains that way, are you?

. . . a bad night last night. I stood at the edge of a cliff but that part was normal. I thought if I had a gun it might startle me out of my state, the thing being it would also startle me out of existence as well, perhaps not such a bad thing. Though to go there for feeling so awful here is no way to travel. Funny thing is I already feel out of existence except I live on. How I got here and how to get out cross my mind but neither is very real. My family stands on the other side, wax. They would not be waiting if they knew what was inside. Lilian thinks she understands but no one does.

. . . The afternoons are long white things with grey splashed over them or black ones depending. Dr. Howze is interested in my talking about our mother and looks skeptical when I tell him I don't remember her so well and that Father and she were happy. I've told him to talk to you since you're older and have more opinions and he says very doctorily he's not interested in history but in what I think. Can you imagine there being such a doctor? Father would start a revolt.

. . . Lilian has gone to London to visit her aunt who will no doubt feed her steaks and cream puffs and entertain her in grand surroundings in extreme contrast to the damp thatched house in which I have landed her.

Dear Lily,

I hope London is what the doctor ordered. I wish the doctor had ordered it for me and that I was there too, though I can hardly imagine what a sidewalk would be like to walk upon or a motorcar door to shut. We think we saw some snowflakes this morning. They went slowly like things in my head, but not as light, floating I mean. Something occurred to me but I think you must know it. I find it hard to say. Sorry to be so this. Don't think I don't know what this has been for you. That is, I don't really but in another way I do and think you must be the most remarkable girl to put up with it. It's as if something got ahold of me at my ankle and pulled me down into a hole and before I knew it I couldn't see anything but how dark it was. The children's eyes are above me and I remember yours even if I don't always see them, dark pools. Today I went down two small hills then up one long gentle slope. How I don't know.

Your Gilbert

At the end of the evening Aunt Tizzy had become a little frayed at the edges. Her lipstick had slid off her mouth, rimming it, and she'd nearly tripped returning from the powder room. She gazed at Lilian with doe eyes, the same eyes Lilian had seen so often on her father after the evening cocktails, on her mother after the nightcap, and seen, too, on Uncle Nat and Aunt Peg when they stopped by summer evenings on the Island. She could picture those droopy eyes — Mrs. Lockwood at Easter, Mr.

Cunningham at Christmas — on nearly everyone she knew in Boston.

You're developing the downturned New England mouth, said Aunt Tizzy.

I blame my ancestors.

Is Mr. Finch making you happy?

It was a ridiculous question, considering the circumstances, and for the first time Lilian understood why her parents rolled their eyes at the mention of Aunt Tizzy's name.

Of course, Lilian said. She'd had wine with dinner, not something she usually did, and felt a haze over everything. He does his best, she said.

Now he is good to the children, said Aunt Tizzy. Children are the nuisance, aren't they? I mean, I love other people's.

He's a sensitive man, Lilian said.

It's the sensitive ones who go under, said Aunt Tizzy, hauling herself up from the table.

S HE TOOK the usual path across the field coming back from the clinic. The sky was grey save for a yellow band of light at the horizon. What was she doing in this foreign country where the days smelled of strange wood burning and the nights were as still as quarries? A wave of fatigue came over her and she stopped. It was a mistake, she knew the moment she stopped, but it was too late. Telling herself she'd rest just a minute, she plopped onto a tuft of grass. It was late spring, and the trees had fuzzed into green. Change in the seasons affected one's spirits. Her breath did not come easily, she clasped her fingers in her lap. Among the bank of trees alongside the field she noticed one tree in particular. How could she have missed seeing it? She'd been coming this way since the fall. It was a big oak set a little apart, with a long low branch extending out a foot off the ground. It seemed to hover in the air without any support whatsoever.

The band of light at the horizon grew narrower and more yellow.

What is it What is it What is it kept going through her mind.

This must be how Gilbert felt, unable to move, in a fish

tank. It seemed as if the trees were watching her. Sometimes there was a glass wall between her and everyone else — she couldn't speak to people on the other side, and when they spoke, it reached her as a sort of muted gurgle, that is, not really reaching her. She wondered if she were catching Gilbert's state of mind. Then she thought of Sally up with a cough the night before, clutching at Lilian's nightgown, trying to be brave. The children were waiting for her. The thought of the children got her to her feet. It occurred to her that this was not enough to get Gilbert to his feet — she supposed it was his knowing they were being taken care of by their mother. What then would make him get to his feet?

At the cottage there was a letter waiting from Dolly who was in London on a visit. Lilian pocketed it amidst the tumult of the children's dinner and baths, and opened it later in her room before changing for dinner. The Vernons were having a wonderful time. Freddie had only a little business and was getting his shirts. Dolly had brought him to the theatre where he slept politely without snoring. And guess who she'd run into? Walter Vail! He was there with an English woman. Did Lilian know that his wife had died? Dolly had certainly put her foot in it. He was due that afternoon for tea at their hotel so Dolly would find out more. Was next Thursday a good day for her to come out and visit?

Lilian felt the sort of throbbing of one suddenly awakened from a nap. Where had they run into each other? Around a corner outside Harrods, coming through a park gate, each with a smiling face and the woman with him standing silently by. What sort of woman would she be?

Thinking of Walter Vail on the same continent disturbed her in a dim way. She went to see that the children were tucked in, and read them a story, causing minor uproars when she altered favorite passages. After dinner she wrote Dolly, saying do come on Thursday. She wanted to hear all the news.

Dolly Vernon could only stay for the day, she had to get back to Freddie.

Let me think what's going on, she said, lifting the pearls at her neck and dropping them with a clink.

They sat on the low sofas in the living room after lunch. Dolly's brother Hugh was interested in one of the Snow girls, though Dolly Vernon couldn't understand why as the girl was mute. Tommy Lattimore sent Lilian his best; he was looking well, and appeared wherever one went. Lilian had received bold letters from him saying Boston was drab, and that he never went anywhere because he knew she wouldn't be there.

Emmett Smith and Reed Wheeler had come back from an Egyptian trip, Emmett knowing more about pyramids now than the experts and Reed with a foreign parasite. Sis and Cap had given a huge Christmas party and Dickie Wiggin came out of his shell to sing. Marian was expecting again, determined to have ten more. Madelaine Fenwick had broken off again with Bill Stockwell, this time for good, and according to her sister was in love with one of her professors. Oh, and Walter Vail! They had run into him near Shepard's Market. He had a woman with him, Dolly thought her pretty in an exotic way, but Freddie considered her too unusual-looking. Walter Vail was dapper as ever. Freddie asked him back to the hotel for a drink later and Dolly said do bring your wife, smiling at the woman, but they both looked uncomfortable and Walter Vail explained that this was not his wife, his wife had died, so they all stood there like idiots. Naturally he didn't show up later. Dolly supposed they weren't smart enough for him. But that was just like him, not to show up, wasn't it?

Lilian had to agree that it was.

Never really understood what you saw in him, Dolly Vernon said. I mean, he's handsome, but . . .

I thought you found him charming, said Lilian, laughing.

Did I? Dolly Vernon shrugged. Can't picture that. Her attention began to wander. Listen, why don't you come back to town with me? Dolly's eyes were bright. Her health was never in the least affected by her diet of cigarettes and cocktails.

Lilian thought of her visit with Aunt Tizzy and how leaving the cottage had disturbed the frail equilibrium she'd found. I don't want to leave the children, she said. Or Gilbert.

Anna can look after the children. And Gilbert — will he even know? Dolly found this clinic business rather ridiculous.

Of course he will. I visit him every day.

I'm worried about you, Dolly Vernon said. She examined her fingernails, then her rings. If you just had a little break . . .

It has been a long winter, Lilian admitted.

You poor dear, said Dolly.

I meant for Gilbert's sake, she said.

Of course, said Dolly, hissing as she inhaled. You know I love him, but honestly. Lilian, he should snap out of it by *now*. It's all in his head, you know. To her, this was proof that nothing was wrong.

Yes, that's what the doctors say. Lilian heard the children in the kitchen playing a rhyming game.

So? Dolly's eyes were wide.

So it's his spirits they're trying to give a boost to, Lilian said.

So give him a martini and be done with it! Look, Gilbert is perfectly sane. Why, he's one of the nicest, sanest men you'll ever meet.

I suppose it's his niceness which is part of the problem, Lilian said.

What if you didn't have money? Dolly sat up, not shy. Do you think factory foremen and bank clerks have nervous conditions?

Are you saying Gilbert is sick because we have a little money? Lilian did not know whether to be angry or amused.

Dolly Vernon sighed, weary of the subject. She stubbed out her cigarette. Something caught her eye out the window in the sunless afternoon. Oh, that's just the sort of hedge we were trying for, she said. How do they get that shape? Do you think one could do the same in Boston? You've got to tell me whom to ask to find out.

GILBERT, feeling better, wrote his college pal Edgar Ames who'd been an usher in his wedding. He felt the need to reestablish contact.

Dear Egg,

I can't remember if it's Madagascar or Tunisia though it's probably someplace else altogether that you are. I am O.K., like a cracked jug with carefully placed clamps, waiting while the glue sets.

Thank you for your letter. Lilian laughed at your interrupting the ceremony and said it was just like you. It was good to see her laugh. Not a great deal of laughing goes on here, inside oneself especially, which is of course the problem. I like thinking of old Egg out crossing continents then at other times I can't figure out much of anything to like thinking about.

But I am much improved. I feel that.

We hope to go home in not too long. Lilian has gotten allergic to England. Finches and Eliots are not meant to live so long away from Boston. Summer does not exist here. Everything turns wet and green and they call it summer. Nurse Metcalfe and I believe it a conspiracy.

If I have to I will finish my treatment, which is what

they call it not I, at one of those places on the North Shore with iron gates and bricks, alongside such as Will Williamson and poor Bud Sears. Mrs. Choate will visit every spring as her spa.

I am proving my salt by spending weekends with Lilian and the children and not scaring the wits out of anyone, including myself. Right now I am fine but the nature of the thing is that you can be in top shape one minute then down in the bleakest depths the next. And for no reason that you can see. They'll probably discover that it's just a matter of vitamins.

Yours,
Gilbert Finch

They'd given him drugs and it made him babble.

I never loved anyone like you, Lily, Gilbert said.

I know. She closed her eyes, then opened them quickly: there was another man's face there.

So kind, Gilbert said. His voice was fading from the medication. So good.

I am not, Lilian snapped.

I don't know how I got so lucky . . . His eyes closed.

Lilian pressed her mouth together, her lower lip protruding, and watched him for a few moments. He looked like something which had been beaten and pounded at till it got soft. She collected her coat and put on her hat, not checking the mirror, and left the tin smell of the clinic. Her walk home was a sleepwalk, for when she arrived back at the tangled thorn bush it was dusk, and she had no awareness of time passing, or of distance having been traveled.

Dear Winn,

We are thinking of coming back. I would have been back a year ago if I was able and now it's up to Kurt Howze to give us the final word which it looks like he will do. Lilian is finding out about places on the North Shore like Hazel Hill and Bartlett's which I know Father does not think highly of, but if it's a question of staying here it will have to do. It has been a strain on Lilian though she wouldn't say and if we're not careful she'll be the one in here not I. After her trips to London her spirits rise but then sink again.

I hope the lawn is in some shape so the children can run about. I have stretches of clear sky and concentrate very hard to see what went into it so I'll be able to conjure it up another time. Best to Edith and Winthrop and yourself.

Love,

Gilbert

V

Irene

THE FINCHES returned from England in 1933 to find all the banks shut. The usualness of Boston seemed valuable and rare, as it had after the war, a feeling Lilian kept for a little while. A few families had been taken down a rung, otherwise everyone was pretty much where he or she had been three years before, except that the children were older and there were more of them.

It was generally agreed that Marian Wiggin spoiled her children, so a birthday party for her daughter, an impossible ten-year-old, was sure to be swell. Lilian stepped into the hazel hallway of the Wiggins' house, holding her daughters' hands in their little white gloves. Underneath their blue coats, the girls wore matching velvet dresses with cuffs. Fay, being older, carried the present and offered it with uncertain arms to Weezie Wiggin who tore the ribbon from the box.

Behind them, Anna carried Porter in her long arms. He slid down his nurse's front and picked up the ivory boar-head walking stick from the stand. He paced deliberately down the hall, inspecting it solemnly. His shoulder blades were sharp under his little white shirt with the crossed straps over it, his head absolutely round and, in the manner of a wooden doll, his legs and arms were as thin as poles. Lilian reflected how strange it was this little boy, so un-afraid and ponderous and confident, had come from her. He gazed with intense curiosity into the Wiggins' drawing room where everyone under ten was screaming at the top of his lungs.

Fay pushed past, eyes gleaming, heading straight to the area of most activity. Below the mantel on the slate hearth, the Vernon boys were spinning tops. She elbowed her way into the circle and crouched down. Lilian found it hard to believe that Fay was her child either.

Marian Wiggin bustled forward. While most of the women were in their day clothes, Marian Wiggin had a dinner dress on. She directed the maid to put the cucumber sandwiches in the library, and told the ladies to go in for drinks or tea. Across the bookcases and vases were pink and white paper accordions, and ribbons festooned the can-dle sconces.

Bobby Putnam was barreling around the room, crashing into chairs, knocking over the younger children. Irene Put-nam rolled her eyes helplessly. Sis Sedgwick stopped him and made him sit down. Lilian noticed Irene Putnam turn quickly, as if someone had tapped her on the shoulder, and the odd thing was not her thinking someone was there, but that her look was so filled with terror. She immediately tried to hide it, striding over to the bar and pouring herself a drink, and concentrated to keep the little square of napkin tucked under her glass.

There was clapping — Sally looked with trepidation up at her mother — and a figure in a clown costume burst from the swinging pantry doors. Some faces regarded him warily, others were enraptured. Sam, the youngest Sedgwick, recognizing the clown from his storybook, ran forward and clasped him around the leg in a desperate hug.

Marian got him for only sixty dollars, Dolly Vernon whispered. She was dressed in a belted tunic with Turkish trim, a new fashion.

Lilian saw with astonishment that she was serious.

The children love him, said Dolly.

I remember when five candles and a blow whistle were sufficient for a birthday party.

Oh, Lilian Eliot, so old fashioned. Dolly Vernon held her elbow cupped in one hand, a cigarette up like a flag in the other. Stop that, Tommy, she called across the room. Let Fay have a turn.

Jane Ives appeared in the door with her stout John and wistful Emily who was as pale and thin as her brother was round and ruddy. Emily, coat removed, ventured forward as far as the frightened children, bumping against Sally Finch. They stared at each other's smocking, stepping from one foot to the other.

The ladies sidled off to the library, keeping an eye on the proceedings through the double doorway.

We go to Venice next month, Madelaine Fenwick Wigglesworth was saying when Lilian walked in. Harry has a conference. Madelaine Fenwick had married the curator Henry Wigglesworth after his wife died, inheriting five stepchildren and adopting the look of a sophisticated fifty-year-old.

Are you staying at the Gritti? said Marian Wiggin, rushing by.

No, we're sponging off the Vails, she said.

Is that Walter Vail? said Dolly Vernon with interest. Ever since their encounter in Shepard's Market, Dolly Vernon had appropriated Walter Vail as part of her property, forgetting for the most part that he'd had anything to do with Lilian Finch, that having been so long ago. Relations were important to Dolly Vernon, but in terms of her immediate experience of the person.

No, said Madelaine Wigglesworth. His parents have a palazzo. Now that she was married to a man twenty years her senior, it was quite natural for her to be going about with the older generation.

Walter Vail. Lilian could almost laugh at the thought. More and more she found she measured her life by how far away she felt from things. Walter Vail seemed the other side of the moon.

The sound of a cranked music box came from the living room. The clown had gotten everyone to sit cross-legged on the floor, each small head tilted back, and was spinning a lamp with cut-outs, making bits of light shaped like horses and birds go around the walls.

Do you know where Walter Vail is now? Lilian said. She cleared her throat at the dryness in the name.

Before Madelaine Wigglesworth could answer, a young woman with the innocent look of a milkmaid charged into the library. Where's the hooch? she said, sounding like a gangster. She drew Lilian over to the bar. Tell me what news you have of Arthur, she said, pouring herself a whiskey. Above her pale eyebrows, braids were laid atop her head, enhancing the peasant impression. Amy Snow Clark looked about fifteen years old.

He's enjoying the tropic climate, said Lilian.

In their youth, Amy Snow had known Arthur well. She smiled and lifted her glass in a toast.

Being Arthur's sister was something no one else was, and Lilian was proud of it, feeling she could understand him better than anyone else. Amy Snow had 'gotten' Arthur too. Lilian told her he was still mostly in Florida, in Palm Beach, hanging around the track more and more and showing up less at the tennis tournaments and the vacation parties of the families from Boston and Philadelphia. His address changed often: care of the Coulters, the Maddens, then of a gentleman named North. Recently, he'd taken an apartment on his own but had evidently moved — Lilian's last letter had been returned.

Bayard loathes palm trees, Amy Clark said. He won't go south of Washington, D.C. Says it's his Yankee blood.

It's his Boston blood, said Marian Wiggin, on her way to replenish the carrot sticks.

I can't see it's a Bostonian characteristic, said Mrs. Wigglesworth. Look at Harry. I can't keep him from dashing off.

Gilbert's not much of a pioneer, Lilian admitted.

Dickie will go, said Marian Wiggin. He just has no curiosity when he gets there.

One could travel alone, I suppose, Lilian said.

The ladies regarded her uneasily.

I guess it depends on where, said Marian Wiggin.

Paris — you could do it, said Madelaine Wigglesworth. Or London. But a woman alone in India — that would be impossible.

Or in Mexico, or Naples, or Russia, said Amy Clark in her gravelly voice. All the interesting places.

Through the doorway Lilian glimpsed Porter standing up in the front row with a frown on his delicate face, disturbed by the scarves coming out from the clown's sleeves.

I think it's the men who would rather not travel alone, said Dolly Vernon, who did not let an opportunity go by of pointing out her husband's devotion to her. Freddie always wants to take me along.

I'm sure it's your company, said Amy Clark with an edge to her voice.

Dolly Vernon ignored it and smiled. They're really such babies, men, she said. One mustn't count on them for too much.

It was odd for Dolly to say. Freddie Vernon was Dolly's sole means of support; her family had taken a beating in the crash.

I feel I can count on Dickie absolutely, said Marian. Then some uncertainty passed over her face. As long as I don't bother him too much.

Cap has the ability to become absolutely stone deaf if he doesn't want to hear what I'm saying, said Sis Sedgwick, wobbling against the sideboard. It wasn't the most promising characteristic for a man who was serving his second term as a Republican congressman, a man who by all accounts was destined for a bright political career.

Jane Ives stirred her tea. I've always quite liked men, she said.

While the cake was being cut in the dining room, Lilian approached Madelaine Wigglesworth. I'm sorry, she said.

Do you know what's become of Walter Vail? I haven't seen him since . . . Her voice trailed off.

You know, said Madelaine Wigglesworth, and her mask seemed to fall and Lilian saw for the first time concern on her face and something bright in her eye. The last I heard of him he was living in London. He's had some bad luck, you know — Lilian nodded, not knowing all of it — but has landed on his feet. He's still doing preservation work over there. But I worry about Walter. Never satisfied with where he is. She shook her head. I imagine it would be terrible to always be so dissatisfied.

Yes, Lilian said, it would.

Madelaine Wigglesworth drifted off. Lilian saw her talking to Elsie McDonnell, and already Madelaine looked lofty and cold again. Lilian wondered at her having been a friend of Walter Vail's, without understanding him, while she, who had a boundless appreciation, had been excluded from his friendship.

She felt a tugging on her skirt and looked down to see Sally's mournful face. I loss my shoe, she said.

That I can take care of, said Lilian, and they went off in search of it.

IT SOMETIMES occurred to Lilian when she was among the children or her lady friends how far off Gilbert's life was from her own. Funny, while he had been sick she felt that they had been somehow closer, the stuff of her days mixed in with the stuff of his. Yet now, despite living in the same house and eating dinners together, something they didn't do while he was at the clinic, their concerns seemed hardly to overlap. Of course they had the children in common, but increasingly that was Lilian's dominion and she merely informed Gilbert of its goings-on.

They'd been back from England, nearly a year now, and Gilbert had been working for Cap Sedgwick whose political career was advancing. At the end of this term he would announce his campaign for the Senate, and Gilbert, who worked closely with him writing speeches, established himself as a behind-the-scenes man, reserved, puzzling to many of the political veterans, yet commanding respect for his sedate gentlemanly manner. He was finding that public service suited his nature. The Finches had a tradition of serving the commonwealth, and despite the lack of financial gain, never a primary concern of Gilbert's, he felt his work worthwhile.

Now when he came home and brooded, it had to do with the contract for the hospital, or the delayed opening of a soup kitchen, so Lilian assumed, since these were the things he talked about at dinner. She could not remember the last time he'd touched her hand in the old way or asked her to forgive him for some small thing, or turned to her to find out what she thought. Not that she was expecting it — no, that time had passed — she was only noticing the change.

He had taken up bird-watching again. At first, Lilian had gone out with him, grateful to see this sign of health. He stood in a russet field, his shoulders in a rumpled canvas coat, waiting for a songbird to fly out of a bush. She tried bringing the children, but they were restless after an hour, fighting with one another and disturbing the birds. On her own she preferred a brisk walk to loitering with binoculars, either that or sitting with a book. So after a while Gilbert took Saturdays to himself, setting off before dawn to catch the screech owls, motoring out to Plum Island or down to Nahant. He would come back with hands cracked from the cold and hair askew from wearing his cap, excited at having seen a gnat catcher or a field sparrow, and would show her examples in the guidebook. Lilian remarked on how ordinary the birds looked.

On weekend evenings they might go to a dinner party together. Yes, but out to dinner one never spoke with one's husband, did one? No, one was farmed out to other people, made to dredge up enthusiasm for discussions of other people's interests — family crests, one's prep school lineage — or other people's misfortunes — would they ever stop talking about poor Mrs. Lindbergh? She and Gilbert would arrive together, and after it was over, would leave with each other, but it seemed as if her own husband were the person furthest away. Lilian couldn't shake the feeling that the life they shared was of the most tenuous construction, and running down the center of it was a gauzy wall which kept them quite separate. They were each within shadowy view but in opposite spaces.

Now and then Gilbert would emerge from his bubble, breaking through the membrane, making something of the old contact with her, but Lilian grew accustomed to his distant manner. She now thought less of the difference from their courtship days, and instead felt it had always been this way.

She discovered anew what she'd learned other times and had forgotten: that something imagined one way could, if given time, turn out to be quite different, without the thing itself having changed a bit. It had happened with places, and things, and people, and she located its happening most specifically with Gilbert's smile. When she'd first met him, the placid set of his mouth had been a beacon to her, but now after years of considering it, the smile seemed a sign of relinquishment, a closed door which would not open, a door which kept something behind it. Perhaps it held back sorrows, she could imagine that. They both had their sorrows, she supposed.

She did her best to look after her own business. She tried to spend an hour or two studying at her desk, following her mother's technique of writing out questions on one page and the answers on another. One day, bent over in her study, she was startled by the sound of Rod clattering a wheelbarrow over the terrace bricks; she looked up at the needlepoint pillow on the opposite chair without recognizing where she was, more absorbed in the life of Saint Theresa than in anything else.

She would have liked to do something more, but what did she have talent for? She'd written verse when she was young, but Arthur was the writer. She thought of the elegant little speech he'd made at Jane's wedding and the wonderful way he had of putting things, with certainty and a particular view. She loved looking at paintings, but could never draw a flower the way it looked, not like Irene Putnam, whose paintings looked like life only better. Dolly Vernon knew how to dress, and Marian Wiggin how to entertain, and even Jane was making use of her education — she'd been to junior college — and was teaching children.

Hildy had once said she had a talent for feeling, and Lilian thought wryly, What could one do with that? She could be a mother and a wife, which she was, but worried that she didn't take the same delight in it the way Dolly or Marian or even Jane in her reserved, matter-of-fact way did. But who knew what went on in their minds. Perhaps they had some of the same thoughts — Lilian simply didn't know.

One evening she went with Irene Putnam to Somerset Maugham's *The Circle*. Lilian didn't go often to the theatre, and felt hypnotized by the action.

You see what I mean, said Irene, and Lilian did.

There was the time she went to the engagement party

for one of the Amory girls and was struck during the toast by the dazed look on the affianced girl's face. Lilian watched the groom whisper something to her and she nodded, in an enchanted stupor.

During these moments Lilian felt an uneasiness. Upon inspection, she saw it involved the extent to which she felt attached to Gilbert. She knew he loved her and that she loved him, but the knowing of it was one thing. She didn't always feel it.

She found herself doubting their early days, the first encounters which had meant so much, the way he had gazed at her. When she had spoken to him then he had stared back with a glassy look, not hearing, and at the time she had thought it was love. Now she wondered if he'd heard her at all, had ever heard, and from there wondered if anyone had heard the things she said.

A feeling lingered in the back of her mind, the notion of having missed something, something important. Had she thought life would be so different?

WITH AN EYE to promoting cultural conversation, the ladies in the luncheon club did not discuss the three M's — marriage, money and men. Thus they heard about Irene Putnam's trip to Rome with the Art League, and were entertained with colorful details of the Vincent Show rehearsals which Marian Wiggin never missed, still, by the time they got to the stewed peaches, the conversation would have settled on the more trivial business of their lives — putting a new stair carpet down, the hiring of a new girl, how young Richard Wiggin compared with little Emily Ives.

All six ladies in the club had attended the Peabody School for Girls and, except for Irene Putnam whose diplomat father had been stationed in Turkey, and whose birthplace was Istanbul, all had been born in Boston.

The luncheon club met each Wednesday at a different house, except for the summer months when the families were in Maine, or at the Berkshires, or on the Cape. At Dolly Vernon's house, they would be fed asparagus nearly grey from being so poached, and they had to fend off the dogs always at one's elbow. Marian Wiggin set her table with good silver and bumpy embroidered linen and served rich sauces, creamed vegetables and *foie gras*. One could always count on Jane Ives for a simple soup and an adequate chicken. At Irene Putnam's you might get something as elaborate as a spinach soufflé or else Irene would forget, and they'd make do with ham sandwiches. Lilian could never get Maureen to make anything more fancy than chipped beef or beef stew or mincemeat pie, which was perfectly fine with Lilian, so that's what the ladies ate at her house.

This Wednesday the ladies had all come out to Brookline to Sis Sedgwick's new house. Sis gave them a tour and all expressed satisfaction with the living room, seeing as it wasn't much different from each of their own living rooms. It was the end of March with the branches bare against a blue and white sky. As soon as the ground thawed Sis and Cap were putting in a swimming pool, an extravagance Sis admitted, given the state of the country.

Hugging themselves without their coats on, they followed Sis out to the back terrace to see the area to be dug. Sis's thin legs poked out from her Scotch plaid kilt. She instructed Jane Ives down on the lawn in her tie shoes which stick meant which corner, and where the deep end would be.

Lilian stood at the edge of the brick terrace and looked back at her friends. Marian Wiggin, pregnant again, sat in an iron garden chair with her feet apart, waving her short arms in the air like seagrass, her fingernails Chinese red. She was distressed at having got fat, but said so with a lift of her eyebrows which showed the opposite. Dolly Vernon looked polished as usual, hair slicked back, wearing a hat with a little peak, her lips magenta. To Lilian, they all seemed more attached to life than she. She was a foot or two further from people than they were from one another.

Irene Putnam arrived late, just as they were sitting down in the light blue and white cameo dining room to the plates of beet salad. On her forehead was a dewy flush and she explained distractedly she'd not noticed the time. No one paid much attention; that was just Irene.

She got a drink from Jonesy as soon as she sat down and lit a cigarette. She fingered her collarbone with a nervous, gloved finger. Strands of her light brown hair had come loose from her hat, and she was wearing the same dark dress with the sweetheart collar she'd had on the last few times Lilian had seen her.

Sis served quail which she said Cap had shot on their last trip to Cheeacaumbe, the Sedgwicks' plantation in North Carolina where jangling hay carts transported cocktail bars from one blind to the next.

Look at the lovely little humps, said Irene as the platter came around.

Dolly said, I don't guess you brought back any fish from the tropics, Jane?

Jane smiled tightly. No, she said, one wasn't allowed to take the fish out.

Dolly Vernon was forever trying to get information out of Jane Ives. Jane rarely spoke of her relations with people. Once Jane had told Lilian she didn't have the least understanding of her husband Jack and didn't really want to. I like the sound of his voice, she said, and the way he looks when he's concentrating on the sail.

Irene Putnam kept smoking throughout the meal, sucking at the cigarette, tapping it even after the ash dropped.

Fishing and killing birds were not the lofty subjects Sis Sedgwick had hoped for during her luncheon. Still, she remained silent, with an engrossed expression, contributing nothing. Fortunately, Irene Putnam brought up the subject of a book she'd been reading. Sis had never understood how someone with so scatterbrained a way of talking could be as smart as everyone said, but now wasn't the time to puzzle over it.

It's wonderful, said Irene Putnam, and awfully entertaining. But one does wonder at the plausibility of it — you know, compared to life.

Marian Wiggin, who felt the words *wonderful* and *entertaining* described life perfectly, shook her charm bracelet and thrust forward her pugdog face.

We've taken the most marvelous house for the summer, she said.

But, Irene went on, I'm not saying our life is bad. I just don't see all the coincidences that are in books, and the adventure, and how people say exactly what they should. I don't see it around.

But that's what one likes to read, Dolly said. I loved the last serial in the *Saturday Evening Post*. Did anyone see it?

Irene frowned. She should have known better than to attempt this. I just wonder why no one writes about it the way it is — you know, with nothing happening.

It could be rather dull, Lilian said.

I suppose, Irene said. Though one does have feelings in

a dull life, which aren't dull, and aren't they worth writing about?

That's where Mr. Shelley comes in, said Jane. And Mr. Keats. They do the feelings.

Sis Sedgwick nodded. The poets were another thing she had never understood. She must have missed them in school, or if she hadn't, she was no less baffled for it. But she was cheered by the turn in the conversation — she would be able to tell Cap they'd discussed poets and writing.

Well anyway, said Irene, and color spread at her very white neck, it was just something I wondered about.

After lunch they took their coffee in the living room. The ladies discussed dresses. No, thank you, Lilian said to Sis passing around the peppermints from S. S. Pierce. Lilian wondered if Marie Curie would have cared about women's coats getting shorter, or if Joan of Arc could have sat for one minute on a flowered sofa in Brookline.

The conversation moved to hats. From there, in natural progression, to shoes, then to Elsie Sears's marriage to the shoe heir and her conversion to Catholicism. This was discussed under the guise of religion.

Then Sis said she'd never really understood about the Virgin Mary, wasn't there something tricky about it? Jane, who'd studied religion, explained how the Immaculate Conception had to do with Mary's conception by her mother, rather than hers of Christ, as was frequently assumed. Still, the virgin part was right.

Why the Catholics make such a big deal about a technicality I don't know, said Marian Wiggin. As far as I'm concerned, the — you know — well, it's no bigger a thing than going to the loo.

It's not as bad as all that, said Dolly.

Irene was staring at the stone geranium urns through the terrace doors. A woman should be able to enjoy it as much as a man, she said.

Lilian gazed at her, hoping she'd go on.

Certainly she can, said Dolly who considered herself up to date on women's emancipation.

You mean the lovely shivery thing? said Sis Sedgwick, thrilled she could add something at last. Oh yes, it is quite something!

The company regarded her with silent astonishment. Sex was a dubious enough place and putting Sis Sedgwick in it was most astonishing.

Irene's cigarette floated through the air in her limp hand, seeking an ashtray, but her face was mesmerized by Sis, and she managed to knock the ashtray to the floor. Irene gazed down at it for a moment: the spilled ashes, the thin slivers of glass. Then she began to pick them up.

Oh, don't bother, Sis said. Just leave it. But she got down on her knees as well. You'll only cut yourself — we'll get Jonesy — oh, my dear, you have!

Irene looked at her hand curiously. Lilian grabbed hold of her — she heard Marian whisper, It was her third — and led Irene by the arm to the downstairs bathroom. Irene was strangely unruffled.

They ran her finger under cold water. Irene washed her hand and dried it recklessly with a towel, refusing a bandage. She threw the towel down and turned to face Lilian.

I — she began — I find it's more and more difficult to say something which matches up with what's in my head. Isn't that silly?

They went back and joined the ladies. When Jonesy came in with more hot water for the pot, she brushed past Irene who jumped in terror. The ladies politely ignored her, but Lilian kept watching her face.

THE FIRE in the fireplace purred like a fan. Lilian sat across from Gilbert.

Not reading? she said.

Gilbert shook his head and stared into the flames. His eyes grew rounder and rounder.

Tired? she asked.

He shook his head in the same way. Twigs hit against the windowpane and the wind howled in the chimney.

What was that? said Gilbert, starting in alarm.

Lilian sat up. I don't hear —

Ssshhh, he said. They both listened.

It's the Greenoughs' dog, he said and heaved himself up. Digging up my bulbs.

Lilian said, I'm sure it's just —

Gilbert went over to the french doors and stared into the night. He rattled the handle and opened it. Scat, he called. Go home. His voice did not carry far in the wind.

It's probably just a raccoon, or a —

Gilbert turned his head around. I don't care what it *is,* Lily, I just want it to get out of my garden and leave me alone.

It happened a few nights out of a month that Gilbert

made the mistake of having one cocktail too many before dinner, or having that extra nightcap afterwards, and he would become rather piffed. Sometimes he even got a little nasty, snapping at her, but she knew it was the alcohol and therefore not his fault. She learned not to blame him. It was more difficult when he stopped making sense altogether which happened sometimes — not frequently, but it did happen. She recognized the signs: his face took on a reddish cast, blooming from within, and his eyes got a hooded puffiness so that when they turned their gaze to you there was some question of their actually seeing you or not.

Gilbert, back in his chair, looked at Lilian in this way.

The book in her lap was a love story, not something she usually read, preferring mysteries or Wodehouse or history, and if she hadn't been reading this the thought would probably not have occurred to her. She didn't spend time thinking about love, but the story made her wonder. It was about a man who loves a woman despite their separation and, more remarkably, without her returning his love or even knowing of the sacrifices and efforts he makes on her account — protecting her husband in battle, seeing her children are safe, saving her from bankruptcy.

During their brief romance the man had been entranced by every aspect of the woman — the way she patted her hair, how she served a picnic, the sound of her laugh, the way she closed her eyes after seeing something beautiful. One wondered, after all this, if it were not the woman, but instead the man who conjured this sort of love.

She looked across at Gilbert. His eyes were making a supreme effort to focus.

You all right? she said.

His pickled face gathered into a frown. Course I'm all right, he said.

It had always been something she took for granted, that Gilbert loved her, and now the unusual thought occurred to her because of this idiotic love story that his love was not necessarily particular to her, that it might have been anyone there in the library with him, anyone else sharing his life, anyone else as long as she was reliable and pleasant and would take care of the house, anyone who would have dinner ready at 7:15, be able to locate his binoculars, leave him alone to his cocktail. It wasn't she who was necessary to him, but rather anyone born in Boston around the time she was born, anyone who dressed as she did, someone preferring a quiet life, a person with money, someone who would leave him alone. And there were other people like that.

She tried to imagine him loving someone else, and wondered how different it would be. But the way he loved came from him, from Gilbert, not from the person he loved, and she had to admit that the fact of her determined his loving not in the least. Why she could have been Elsie or Madelaine or Marian or Nita Russell for all the effect she had on him. She felt quite superfluous.

I'm going to bed, she announced, standing up.

You do that, said Gilbert. He wasn't looking at her anymore, his attention was back on the blackened fireplace. I'm going to read some more, he said, though his book was nowhere in evidence.

THE GENERAL consensus had always been that Irene Minter Putnam, though pretty and talented, was a little strange, and Lilian would have continued thinking so, too, if she hadn't taken the water color class one summer in high school at the Museum of Fine Arts and gotten to know Irene then. Irene never seemed to pay attention, but remembered everything the teacher had said, mostly to disagree, something Lilian admired.

Despite the accomplishments of Irene's diplomatic parents, or perhaps because of them, Lilian's parents were not close to the Minters. Mrs. Eliot found Irene's mother a fright who shouted at dinner parties and wore low dresses, so didn't think it a surprise that her daughter was odd. That Irene had talent meant less than the fact that Mrs. Minter was half-Italian. Mr. Eliot thought the debonair Paul Minter an ass. But Lilian had always found Irene odd in an interesting way, with her marble-smooth skin and glassy black eyes and quick reactions. The Minters' house on Charles Street had European touches with a round marble hall in front and a trellised grape arbor in back where they used to eat outside on Sundays. After Irene married Bobby Putnam, she brought those European touches to their own house on Beacon Street, putting Spanish iron railings in the hall, growing lemon and olive trees, and draping rugs over the tables. Lilian liked the light and the paintings and wished she had the courage to try it herself. She made an attempt at draping some fabric around a hassock and hanging tassles off the valances, but it clashed with the rest of the room and she took it down before any of the ladies saw. Though she did manage a simple lemon tree on a gravel tray in the front hall which to her carried an exotic air.

Lilian called on Irene Putnam one day and found her not unusually in a distracted state. It had been a year since Sis Sedgwick's luncheon when she'd cut her hand and seemed not to mind, and since then Irene Putnam had been carried out of a few dances and discussed now and then over tea. She'd spent the past Christmas in bed with the shades down. One day she would be raccoon-eyed with worry, and on another intent in her old way, as if a thin white flame were consuming her.

Today she was wearing the cornflower smock she sometimes painted in, though her easel was not out. She was biting her fingernails. Lilian convinced her to send for some tea, but Irene went to the bar shelf and made herself a gin.

I can't seem to get anything done, she said. She laughed. Her face fell.

What exactly . . . ? Lilian said.

Irene drifted about the room, fretting at her wrist sleeve. Little Julie — she's — I suppose it's not something I ought to — but you know how girls are — it's the boys I don't understand — but she's only seven for God's sake — I don't — oh, oh have some tea, Lil — so rude of me, let me . . .

I'm perfectly fine, Lilian said.

Yes, said Irene, smiling at her. You are. She sat down. Didn't Lilian ever feel that she was, how could she say it, in the wrong place?

It stirred something in Lilian, the thing which didn't match up with the world. But she was more struck by Irene's bedraggled state and wanted to help her friend.

Why, no, she said.

Irene looked at her helplessly. I don't know what it is lately — she laughed in a quick high way — oh, but how are you? She leaned forward, elbows and knees meeting. And your mother, how is she?

Mrs. Eliot's health had been frail. It had affected her parents to such an extent they were unaware of it. She's fine, Lilian said, the only answer she ever gave to questions about her mother.

Please send her my best, said Irene. She had no idea of Mrs. Eliot's real opinion, and always expressed warmth toward her, disturbing Lilian who hated unequal things.

Irene stood up and poured another drink. What is that noise? she said impatiently.

What noise?

That buzzing.

I don't hear any —

I heard it the other day playing tennis, Irene said. Like crowds, or something buzzing. She stopped when she noticed Lilian's expression.

How's Bobby? Lilian said, trying for a lighter note.

But Irene looked as if she'd been asked to solve a mathematical equation. She went to the desk drawer, a lovely yellowish desk painted with palm trees and Indian figures, and pulled out a pile of travel brochures. He wants to go on a trip together, Irene said, as if this were the idea of an insane person. He thinks it would be *good* for me.

Oh, but a trip would be wonderful, Lilian said.

Irene handed Lilian a brochure with a distinct lack of interest. Some island, she said. The only good thing about it is the name of the hotel: the Blue Ruin. Irene laughed. Like me.

She downed her drink. Don't you hear? A wild look passed over her face. There it is again. She turned to Lilian with her black eyes. I'm sure you think I'm quite mad, she said.

THAT SPRING Lilian Finch brought the girls to Florida for a week in March. They picked up shells in the
wet sand and ate pineapple sherbet for dessert. She called
the number she had for Arthur a few times and finally got
a Hispanic gentleman who told her that Mr. Eliot was not
aquí. He hung up before Lilian could leave a message. They
were not so far from Palm Beach and Lilian felt his close-
ness but tried not to feel the keenness of it. The girls helped
see to that.

Later that same spring Irene Putnam went with her husband down to the Blue Ruin. Everyone heard about the
trip. Bobby Putnam told the story in his deep Adam's apple
voice, shortening it each time as he became more adept
with the important points. Lilian heard the earliest version
and was glad for the details, finding that they revealed more
than Bobby Putnam was aware.

They had had to take a number of planes to get to the
island, each aircraft shrinking in size till the last tiny one
landed them on a short airstrip. They rented a car and
drove over a straight dry road seeing no cars going the
other way, heading to the north of the island. The land was
flat, dusted over with white, with low brush, and Irene said

how much she liked it. They stopped and got out of the car
to watch the sun go down. Bobby Putnam leaned against
the car, arms folded, squinting, wondering if they should
try to get a boat tomorrow. Irene stood in the scrappy
weeds, still in her wool dress but bare-legged, having taken
off her stockings. It occurred to Bobby Putnam that they'd
not been alone together since the children had come, at
least it seemed so, and he thought of how Irene was a
different girl from the one he'd married, a woman now he
supposed, and it struck him, seeing her away from Boston,
though he couldn't have said how, how different she was.
A traveler's weariness hung over them, pale and rumpled,
and they felt slightly disoriented.

That night they ate in the dining room with the other
guests, a few small families, a pair of elderly sisters, a middle-age couple, and another couple their age. The usual
group. They tried the local cocktails then fell back on their
usual gin. Bobby Putnam was a gin man, and it was
through him that Irene had taken it up. She had made an
effort earlier in the month — Lilian had known about this
— to cut down on the drinking, and her doctor had given
her some pills to help her sleep, but she found that it hadn't
improved her mood, in fact quite the opposite, so she'd
taken it up again. Bobby Putnam had encouraged her, they
were here to have fun after all. He thought drinking would
make her feel better, it did him. He wondered afterwards if
the period of abstinence might not have thrown off her
system.

The next day was pleasant enough, as far as Bobby Putnam could remember. They spent the morning looking

around, taking a walk on the beach, and lunched at a little striped restaurant overlooking the reef. In the afternoon, he'd gone to try the golf course. He supposed he shouldn't have left her alone, but how was he to know? He got into a foursome. It was a scruffy course but the greens were well kept and the holes were arranged around bodies of water. The game lasted a long time. When he got back to the hotel it was nearly dark, and Irene was outside their cottage at a table with no light on, having a drink. She had already had a few. The wind had picked up — they got the Atlantic winds on the east side — and the waves were crashing close by. The palm fronds blew around like rattling venetian blinds. She was wearing a pale yellow dress — Bobby rubbed his eyes behind his butterscotch glasses as he told the story, exhausted by the thought. Her figure in the dark was luminous, without a head or limbs.

After dinner they went to a little bar to dance, a green place with nets and colored beads, down the hill from the hotel. They were on vacation, so was it so unusual they'd had a lot to drink? The couple their age from the Blue Ruin dining room nodded hello and asked the Putnams to join them. They'd passed each other in the lobby and now properly introduced themselves. He was English and his wife was, too, though she looked Persian or Lebanese and spoke with a slight accent. Very attractive, said Bobby Putnam, and educated. The husband was an archaeologist or anthropologist — Bobby Putnam could never keep it straight. Irene was friendly and curious, the way she got after a few drinks, and to keep herself steady was leaning against the Englishman as she asked him questions. He didn't mind, but the wife did. Bobby Putnam took it upon himself to distract the wife, you know, and pulled her up to dance, and in no time she had forgotten what her husband was doing. How long they danced he wasn't sure — with calypso music one song bangs on into another — but it hadn't been too short a time.

Suddenly, for no reason that Bobby Putnam could see, Irene tore past him out of the bar, a pale streak in her fluttery dress — Lilian knew the dress, they'd bought it together, she remembered there were small orange buds on the bodice — and when Bobby Putnam followed her out, not *right* away, not hurrying, he knew Irene's hysterics and didn't want to get caught up in them, he spied her across the stone square. She stumbled near a row of flipped boats lined up by the beach. Black palm shadows fanned across the square lit up by one ancient streetlight. Irene hit at him when he came near her and tripped in her sandal heels, cursing him. Oh, she was in a bad way, said Bobby Putnam, very tight, and Lilian saw that his eyes were troubled. So it had affected him after all, Lilian thought. But it was the only time she saw the look. Afterwards, telling the story, there would be a hardness in his eyes, as hard as his straight teeth, as smooth as his dry jaw. She did not wish Bobby Putnam ill, but she wanted to see signs of his wife in him; Lilian wanted to see something in him she could like. She saw it only that one time. Men, she thought, were expert at covering up — women showed more on their faces — though she wondered if the effort of covering up didn't secure the disturbance and preserve it.

Yes, she was in a very bad way, said Bobby Putnam,

she'd banged up her knee, skinned her chin, and there was
blood down the front of her dress. She was ranting about
nothing, about the moon and I can't even remember what
— Lilian wanted to press him but realized he'd never listened to Irene, not really — her eyes were blazing and
whirling, he said, those black eyes. She was drunk! And
then she got onto this idea about wanting to call the children and working herself into a state about Julie's being —
oh, I don't know what, she wanted to call them to see if
they were all right, she acted as if she'd just discovered they
were in some kind of danger. She was hysterical, ridiculous, and when I put my arms around her to help her
up, she wouldn't budge, but she'd gotten so thin it wasn't
hard to lift her. I told her the children were fine. They
can do just fine without us, I said, and she looked at
me in a relieved, close way. I remember because it was
like the eye of the storm the way she was suddenly still
and lucid and very nearly reasonable, and she said, Do
you really think so? in a soft tone, as if that's what had
been troubling her all along, so I said, Of course I do,
encouraging her, you know. I should have said something
else, I see now.

In the morning they slept past breakfast, had a basket
lunch made, and drove to an empty beach. Irene was quiet;
they were both hung over. She wrote the children a letter,
and drew a pen and ink sketch of the bay. Bobby Putnam
had asked the English couple to join them, not feeling they
had anything to do with the hysteria of the night before,
and maybe they didn't. They arrived, the man in khaki, the
woman with a midnight blue scarf around her head. They

poured drinks under the umbrella and chatted. Irene had the look of wanting to tell her husband something, he thought of it afterwards, or maybe he'd imagined it. But he was tired after lunch and fell asleep. When he woke the sky was clouded over, and he saw it was past his reserved golf time. Irene said she didn't want to leave — it was so peaceful there, she said — so Bobby Putnam caught a ride back with the English couple.

He played only nine holes. Not feeling on top of the world — all the sun he guessed — he had a drink at the clubhouse with a fellow from Glen Cove who it turned out knew Irene's family. Very bright girl, the fellow said. Bobby Putnam liked him for his complimenting his golf shoes. When he got back to the cottage it was still light and the rooms were as they had been that morning, only straightened up by the maid. He looked around outside and there was no sign of Irene, not at the table, not on the beach path. He went up to the lounge to see if she was there, but found only sunburnt guests looking forgotten and a bartender shoveling at ice. At the desk he asked if they'd seen Mrs. Putnam. A headache throbbed at his temples, he was annoyed having to look for her. The woman listened to a voice through the door behind her, and said with some uncertainty that they'd not seen her. Their car was not in the lot. He borrowed a bicycle and rode through the dusk down to the beach where they'd been. Coming around the corner, he saw the car parked among the curving tree trunks. He rested the bicycle against the fender and called her name. It was quiet on this side of the island, the western side, and the water was flat, lit up as bright as the sky, a flat blue blending into pale pink, brighter at the horizon.

Her towel was still on the beach, beside the picnic basket and her crumpled sailor pants, and the big bag with sun lotions and combs and paper pads and books lay collapsed nearby. She always brought two or three books to the beach as if she were going to read them all, as if she had the time, but once there would simply stare at the water or draw lazy sketches. He looked down the beach to the left, where the sand dwindled to a sliver; he walked up to the little point on the right and looked around the cove. Irene! he called. His head was pounding and he felt the beginnings of panic. He was used to the troubling presence of Irene, but her absence was something new, more troubling. And it was only then, he said — Lilian thought it delayed of him not to have thought of it before — that he realized how serious it might be.

Later he'd found the letter she'd written to the children, slipped between the pages of her book.

Dear Pets,
    The beach I'm sitting on has white sand and the one next door has black sand. Right now Daddy is swimming in a big green wave. At night they give us porpoises in our drinks. At night I miss my babies most of all. Bobby, you must look after Julie and Blair. Your mother loves you very much.
    She always will.

Bobby Putnam shook his head. Then he spoke with some animation about the search teams, the Coast Guard patrols, and the lackadaisical police department. They looked for her for a week. Nothing, he said.

* * *

Everyone in Boston discussed the case, shaking their heads, refusing to believe it of her. Yes, she was troubled, but *this* wasn't like her. Lilian never said how it was exactly right, and that it fit Irene Putnam perfectly, one part of her at least, but why should she? They wouldn't have understood Lilian any better. Now and then the idea was revived that she had run off, and was still alive somewhere, but Lilian knew better about that too.

Within the year Bobby Putnam was married again, to one of the Lothrop cousins from Sherborn, a riding intimate of Sis Sedgwick's who didn't have the least interest in art.

LILIAN WATCHED the men on the tennis court, high noon, the voices of the spectators low in the summer air. Gilbert, in a sun hat and limp shorts, held his racket loosely waiting for a serve. Behind him through a net was a field of Queen Anne's lace, goldenrod, and bay bushes with a path cut through to a house farther back. Three children appeared, carrying rackets as large as themselves, and stopped in dismay when they saw the court occupied by grownups.

It was the semifinals of the Island tournament. Gilbert's partner, Cap Sedgwick, bent at the waist like a long insect, intent on every shot, looked flushed with exertion. Their opponents, a father and son, the younger about seventeen, both with a redhead's complexion, were people Lilian had never seen. Guests of the Amorys', someone said, from New York. They were winning.

There was a low rumble from the area of the green benches while the teams switched sides. Lilian sat a little apart, wrapped in a sweater, preferring not to chat. Since Gilbert's improvement, her attention had been taken up by the children, and yesterday Sally and Fay had gone on their first real trip away, visiting their Finch cousins in Camden where Edith had family, woodsy poets and retired lawyers, and the big house with only quiet Porter organizing his bug collection was larger and more still. Small changes made a big difference in her life. It was no wonder she was thinking so often of Irene.

She found it turned her thoughts in the direction of herself. She'd woken early that morning, and later, there'd been a card from Tommy Lattimore in Greece, and a letter from Jane Ives in Spain, putting her in mind of faraway places. She daydreamed, and became absorbed by a butterfly jigging by.

She wondered if anything more could possibly happen in her life — not that so much had, but everything seemed so airtight, all the seams sewn up. There was little space for anything new. Yes, the children would keep growing. Fay would become more accomplished at talking back, Sally at staying quiet, and Porter would have to be fitted for glasses. One day each of them would — she leapt ahead — marry and go off, but that would be their lives. A small round of clapping rose around her — Lilian joined in regardless of whom it was for. She thought of the white hall of the children's hospital where she still went once a week to read to the children. They sat up in the middle of their beds, little statues, perplexed, waiting like small animals, looking on with resignation at a leg being bandaged or an arm pricked. They had yet to develop the outrage of an adult, or the bitterness, and their faces shone with the trust of those who believe life will turn out well.

Lilian watched the butterfly, straining toward it as if toward something which mattered to her. What was it? She felt all . . . padded. Everything in her life was soft. It was not an extravagant life, they did not overindulge. They ate simple food, slept on simple beds, were satisfied with a reading evening. But at bottom there was a cushion. Sometimes she felt ashamed of it. Earlier in the summer, going out to the Wiggins' in Beverly Farms, she took the train and passed through North Station where the hobos were out along the tracks, black-toothed, sooty, wearing caps, some wrapped in blankets like cocoons, some sleeping, and wondered how it was she happened to be where she was and not there.

The ball thumped into the net. Gilbert did not show any signs of minding that they were losing. Cap, however, despite his Yankee reserve, was used to elections, and winning, and he stiffened his jaw and slammed his long-armed serves into the net. Their opponents remained steely, exchanging pinched nods. Now and then the father snapped an order at his son.

Lilian followed the butterfly, it was way off now, a pale speck making an uneven line, visible against the pine trees one moment, then disappearing against the white sky. She'd known things like that in her life, compelling, distracting things, they tantalized her, but finally were too delicate to hold. They disappeared in an instant. It had been a long time since she'd been bewitched by something that way. What a thought to have! I may be a thoughtful woman, but I'm not a dreamy one.

That afternoon she took Porter down to Victor's stand for an ice and sat with him on the wall by the memorial fountain. Old Mr. Lamont, who usually did not distinguish one woman from another, walked by and told her she looked a vision today. She had let her skin get dark and it showed up against her white dress. Later, picking up a book at the library, Clara Biggs who was not one for small talk seemed genuinely surprised at how she'd changed since the summer before. It was funny how everyone assumed that happiness made one look well when it could be the opposite. Suffering refines, Aunt Tizzy used to say. Feeling anything strongly gives one the look of being alive.

In the evening she and Gilbert went to the Searses' for cocktails, and Lilian shook hands with the man who had beaten her husband at tennis.

His name was Hugh Poor. He was tall and half-bald, with a delicate nose and a face pink from the sun. He spoke with a slight English accent, as if he'd lived abroad. I hear you're an old friend of my cousin Walter's, he said.

Lilian couldn't think of anyone by that name.

Walter Vail, the man said.

Oh, she said. Yes. She liked the sound of that, *an old friend of Walter Vail's.* A long time ago. You're his cousin?

My mother was a Vail, he said with a penetrating look.

And how is — ?

Gilbert came over with the interested expression he got when he wanted to go home.

Hugh is Walter Vail's cousin, said Lilian in a strange, high voice. Gilbert had known of Walter Vail from the years before their engagement.

You know Walter? said Hugh Poor.

Can't say I do, said Gilbert.

Well, he's coming day after tomorrow, said Hugh Poor.

Here? said Lilian.

That's right, said Hugh Poor, not surprised. He's meeting up with some friends who have a splendid boat, and they're continuing up the coast to Dark Harbor, I think.

Gilbert made his departure signal.

It was nice to meet you, Hugh, said Lilian.

Ta-ta. I'll give your regards to Walter.

Do, she said, and smiled. One could always smile and have it mean so little.

As they were getting into their car, Lilian said, I seem to remember a time when the mention of Walter Vail's name inspired a certain reaction in you. She borrowed the teasing tone Arthur used, not bringing it off.

My young and foolish days, said Gilbert. Later, as if admitting defeat, he said, What's the matter?

Nothing.

Not having the girls around has given you a turn, I think.

I'm sure you're right, she said.

On Monday morning, Porter went down to Boston with his father to meet Aunt Tizzy, who was taking him to the pony show. They would return the following weekend when Gilbert came back up. The girls were still in Camden a few more days. So when Walter Vail arrived on the Island the next evening, a windy night in August, Lilian Finch was quite alone.

VI

Aunt Tizzy

H E WAS there a day and a night before he came to see her.

She had been in the attic all morning, the house being empty, batting through the cobwebs. As she ducked past the eyelid window, she saw his figure cross the lawn, striding straight-backed, not swinging his arms. She stood still, clutching an old canvas cushion cover. She had hoped for a glimpse of him, and maybe this was enough, for she recoiled from more. But she stood up and went downstairs. As she did, she composed a placid face.

You *are* here, he said, smiling broadly, coming up the piazza steps. He put his arms out and enveloped her briefly in them, not exactly awkward but somehow stiff, greeting her as an old friend — wasn't that what she was now?

I heard you were coming, she said, at first unable to look at him. They stepped into the sun, talking cheerfully, exchanging news of their families. He was thinner, not more portly as she'd often imagined, with a good haircut, and was wearing the same sort of shirt Gilbert wore with a soft tennis collar. His eyes looked older, but otherwise he seemed hardly changed. She told him so.

I've come to take you away, he said in the old familiar way. We're going on a day sail.

Oh, she said. When? She wanted to seem as if she had other more engaging things to do.

Come on, he said, ignoring her pose. We leave in half an hour. I've come to fetch you. He started down the steps of the piazza.

All right, she said, letting go the pretense. She needed some things and would meet him down at the float. She dashed back into the house and paused in indecision over which sweater to bring and changed her shoes and snatched up her one and only hat.

The *When and If* was a lovely boat, pale grey, with a brass overlaid steering wheel, a mammoth boom and stylish people on deck.

I am sorry your husband's not here, said Walter Vail, and Lilian realized that for all their talk of children, of her father's retirement, and of his mother's poor health, they'd not mentioned each other's spouses. But then Walter Vail and Gilbert Finch occupied different orbits.

As soon as they were under way, Walter Vail settled her with his friends, withdrew against the gunwales and left her to them. His friends were lively, speaking more of world events than dinner parties. One couple had just been to Europe. One of the men had met a movie star and told an amusing anecdote. As she sat across from Walter Vail in the cockpit, brushing back the hair swirling around her face, she noticed how unaffected she was by him. Her skin was thicker and the person within was protected now. Of course, she thought, I'm a married woman with three children, of course I'm not going to think of him in the same way. He was as charming as before, his brow alive when asking a question. He leaned back to put his face full in the wind, and leaned forward suddenly to save Lilian from a rope being winched. His friends asked about the Island, treating her as a local historian, and she came up with the somewhat fuzzy facts her father had pronounced so often. At one point she mentioned her maiden name and the fellow in the striped shirt, the one who'd met the movie star, asked her if she were any relation to one Arthur Eliot.

Actually, said Lilian, lifting the Eliot chin, Arthur is my brother.

Really, said the man blandly. He's also a crook.

Gerald! said one of the women.

I'm sure it's no surprise to Mrs. Finch, said Gerald.

I don't know what you mean, Lilian muttered.

Oh, your brother befriends people, borrows money from them and then, well, leaves town. He spoke with a jaded air. Didn't you know?

Lilian said not a word.

Gerry, that's enough, said the catlike woman folded in a wrap. She had a deep, menacing voice. It's too tiresome.

You don't know how tiresome, actually, said Gerald. Of course, I don't blame you, Mrs. Finch. I hope you don't think I was.

The woman stood up and went to the bow.

God, she's going into a sulk. I better make rapid amends. He looked over his shoulder at Lilian. Do please pardon me, he said coolly.

Lilian did not at first look in Walter Vail's direction, and when she did he appeared not to have heard anything. What a stranger he was to her really, despite the private things between them. It was as if he were assuming the role of an old friend as some kind of duty. Lilian wondered why he bothered.

That night she was pressed by Walter Vail to have dinner at the Amorys' and did, sitting beside Hugh Poor and listening to stories of England where he'd gone to school. She was grateful the man named Gerald and the people from the boat were not in evidence. The last time she'd heard from Arthur was a raspy phone call at Christmas — he had asked for a loan — and the depiction of his life by Gerald had an eerie ring of truth to it. She was fearful of hearing more. She clung to the notion of his being unlike other people, of his special talent, and did not want to see him as someone not worthy of admiration.

Walter Vail spent most of the evening with his ear tilted toward old Mrs. Amory who knew much of society in New York as well as Boston. Elsie McDonnell sat on his other side, looking abandoned.

When it came time to go Lilian said goodnight to the general audience and Walter Vail leaped up from a wicker armchair as if he'd only just remembered to look after her. Lilian thought him an altogether curious fellow.

I'll walk you home, he said.

Oh, it's close.

I'd like the air, he said, and opened the door.

She had known him little enough and over a long enough period of time for her to recall their other encounters and compare them with this one. Now they were walking on a summer road shady with night leaves, not on tilted city streets lit up with snowfall. The stillness was different. The darkness of the Maine sky thickened over by clouds was different from the sky with the pink glow of the Common. They walked down the middle of the road, feeling the tar still warm through their shoes. Like his old self, Walter Vail asked questions of general interest — what had become of her Boston friends, what did they do here on the Island by way of entertainment, whom did she see. News of himself was treated as something completely uninteresting, so Lilian found out little of his circumstances. She said she'd heard of him over the years, of his wife's death — at this he merely nodded, his dark profile tightening at the mouth — heard that he'd remarried. Well, that's over now too, he said.

At the house they stopped by the side piazza steps. There were no lights in any windows, but something luminous from the harbor, or the stars behind the clouded sky made for enough light to see. He asked her about the house, admiring the gutters, and she told him they'd bought it after Sally was born when they'd become too many to stay at the house on the cove with her parents. They sat down on the steps, facing out. She found herself telling him about Irene Putnam and her disappearance. Walter Vail's face, atilt, took on a sympathetic expression, wincing like someone braced to be hit.

It's hard to lose . . . , he began, but trailed off.

Very starkly there appeared to Lilian like dark birds on the lawn all the losses she had known since she'd last seen Walter Vail — Irene Putnam, then Hildy, who'd died in

June after months of wheezing in a metal bed, and further back all those years, thinking of the boys who hadn't come back. Lilian told him about Forrey Cooper and the memorial fountain in town. He said he'd had a friend who'd never come out of the Black Forest. Staring out at the lumpy bank of raspberry bushes at the lawn's edge, Walter Vail reached over and placed his hand on top of Lilian's which looked like a beige glove forgotten on the step. As he talked he kept his hand there, enveloping her fingers, tightening his clasp, talking on with no reference whatsoever to what his hand was doing. The pressure increased, and Lilian felt she was coming to know him again. His self was returning. And then it wasn't just he who returned, but herself as well. She felt the air on her face.

The usual stuff of her life fell away, tumbling down past the lawn's edge, dropping off the cliff, leaving her and Walter Vail alone in the world. The space around them seemed complete. Their talk grew warmer, easier, and they stayed on the steps for a long time. When they stood up and went into the house, they were one pale shape with two heads, and it had gotten quite late.

In the morning Walter Vail was gone.

So THIS, she thought, is how my life turns out: that there are slivers into which I pack my greatest feeling, that the moments with this skittish man who appears now and then in my life are to have more power than all the days with my husband. Of course, the precariousness made her feeling more intense, she knew, but knowing did not lessen it. She scorned herself. I've never been one of those foolish people taken up with romantic notions. I have my feet on the ground, anyone would say so; I have always been a reasonable woman. But then she would drift back into reverie.

There was an extra room inside her now, a wing built off the usual rooms, with a chaise and a window looking out to a tree, where she kept their time together, and when it was cold she warmed herself at the fire wavering in the grate, and when it was stifling she stood at the open window looking at the rolling vista, feeling the fresh wind. It was their place, and in it she was set dreaming.

Was there harm in holding on to it? Really, she thought, what damage could it do now?

She sat at her dressing table in her slip and pulled at the hairpins. Her hair fell onto her shoulders, slipping over skin. She fluffed at her hair, releasing the smell of shampoo. She turned her face from side to side looking in the mirror and sat up, twisting her torso to see the curve.

You ought to send the children off more often, said Gilbert. He had returned, wilted from his week in town, and remarked on her improved mood. They were dressing for dinner and he patted her hand as he shuffled past. She seized up, comparing the patting of her hand to the clasping of it by another. Then she remembered, in a strange rambling back, how Gilbert Finch had clasped her hand too, as they drove in Scotland with the leaves blurring by, and the neat filing away of feelings crumbled into chaos. She briskly brushed her hair.

With the children home, life continued as usual — there were tennis lessons, picnics on Molly's River and afternoon sails on the Ives' boat. And in the weeks that followed Lilian continued to daydream.

Gilbert Finch remained in his usual place, steady and unchanging, blending in with his surroundings. He was present and accounted for, but his form faded in and out of view. Sometimes she felt she were married to a ghost.

Each evening he pulled radishes from the garden, and in the cool kitchen smelling of gas, sliced white nicks in the rosy red and chopped ice off a block and arranged it all in a bowl. He sat out on the piazza in a slatted green chair, a drink within arm's reach, reading his book. Through the pine trees, people next door could be heard on the tennis courts, the ball batting dully. He was interrupted by the children, Fay at the screen door asking him where Anna had gone with Sally. He did not know. Had he seen them?

Not recently. They were supposed to be going to the Cobbs', said Fay with a ten-year-old's exasperation. He said he knew nothing about the Cobbs and popped a radish into his mouth. Fay stamped her foot. Pa, she said. He looked at her, and saw a brow riddled with lines. Why was it that the females around him were perpetually worried? How he wished they would leave him out of it. There was never anything he could do. He knew this with such clarity, why didn't they?

They moved back to Boston and the fall season began.

Back among the yellow leaves and the all-day rain Lilian felt the glow of her memory dim and the construction of her wing grow shaky. Sometimes it was difficult to reach it — as if the light had blown in the hall, or the door were jammed. Or once there it might seem smaller than before, the ceiling lower, the air oppressive.

She had had no word from him.

She did not expect a letter, though some unreasonable part of her did, and the whole of her suffered as a result. She relived the pains of years before, mortified to be repeating them. Just one letter would placate her. It was not asking for much! And yet, with a start she was aware of asking for something.

There had never been any question of the future. He had not mentioned anything — it was absurd to think of it — and even if he had, well, there were her children, and she was married to Gilbert.

With dissatisfaction the memory began to alter, and the room darkened from a bright place to a blacker one: there was a strange burnished light, thunder threatened outside, the curtains looked dingy, and the fire smoked sullenly.

She went out her usual amount, determined that her outward life not be changed. At a number of visits she found herself drawn to old Mrs. Amory simply for the fact of her having had the tête-à-tête with Walter Vail that night on the Island. She took up books about architecture and read them with interest.

Over the following months, and then over the years, she heard news — rumors, facts, she was never sure — he was living in New York, he'd taken a flat in London, he was reconciled with his wife, he was engaged to a girl from Minnesota. But what did any of it matter? Lilian knew what she had to do, she had done it before.

The fire in the wing cooled over the months and eventually over the years, doused with reason and resentment and resignation. The floor rang hollowly. It became finally a place of sorrow, and after a while she did not go there anymore.

IT WAS AUTUMN, late October, and the leaves lay in a
sea around the house on Curtis Road. Mr. Eliot set out
on his usual walk after Sunday lunch, leaving Mrs. Eliot
with her needlework and sherry.

He crunched his way along the gravel driveway and
turned onto the trail between the Nathans' and the Colchesters', under the yellow archway of trees, kicking dead
leaves, thinking of the radio show he'd listen to that evening. A bird flew by, rising and falling, showing a back
stripe. His son-in-law had taught him it was a yellow
shafted flicker. The children always grew excited when
they saw pheasants, and Mr. Eliot liked to explain that they
were not indigenous to America — he knew something
about birds himself — but had been brought over from
Asia. He recalled one incident when his little grandson
Porter had gone chasing after one, running into the woods
like a wild creature, then realized with a jolt that it hadn't
been Porter at all but his own son Arthur, thirty-some years
ago. The confusion in his memory made him uneasy, and
he was glad he'd not said it out loud to someone. He put it
out of his mind. The last time he'd heard from Arthur was,
oh, must have been three years ago, Margaret had gotten a

birthday card from Florida, and a few days later came the letter asking for money. He'd sent Arthur a portion of what he'd asked for and heard nothing more.

The sky was blue between the sharp clouds; the light changed when the sun flashed down, spotting everything in patterns then fading when a cloud came overhead. Feeling his belt a little tight across his belly, he regretted not passing on Rosa's bread pudding.

Mrs. Eliot used to accompany him on these walks, especially after the children were gone, but in the last few years the cold bothered her more, and with her joints seized up, she had to stay inside. He'd been unable to coax her out for many years, but he was content to walk alone.

Through the spaces in the thinned-out trees he could make out the tiered garden at the Colchesters'. It didn't look as if anyone was home. The rosebushes had been bound with burlap, and hay was packed along the garden beds, ready for frost.

Mr. Eliot wore his good pants — he always dressed for Sunday lunch — but his jacket was the old one from Abercrombie's he wore every fall. It was, Margaret had pointed out, her forehead wrinkling with the extreme pity she reserved for clothes, beginning to tatter at the collar. Mr. Eliot said he liked it that way.

He crossed the lane and continued along the trail toward the Olneys'. He passed a group walking the other way — it must have been some of the Fenwick children, the boy looked just like Diana. He nodded, never could remember their names. Hello, Mr. Eliot, said one of the girls, carrying a baby. Was that Lilian's friend? No, she'd been taller, he thought, and remembered oddly that that was where Lilian had found that disagreeable fellow, the one who was killed in the war, wasn't it? And Lilian had taken it badly. Margaret even worried about her getting over it, but of course she would, and did. He had three Finch grandchildren to prove it. Extraordinary, the odd thoughts which came into one's head.

At the Olneys' pond there was a large congregation of Canada geese covering the sloping bank. He saw the swans on the other side, white curves in the shadows, and just as he arrived at the trail's opening, a pair of mallards swooped down. He'd have to tell Margaret: the mallards were still there.

Smoke rose from the Olneys' chimney. As he passed around the back he saw Ellen Olney waving from the kitchen window. She popped her head out the back door.

Tell Margaret I've got her book, she called in a high voice. Since Trip Olney's death, Ellen Olney had become more loquacious.

Will do, he shouted, not coming any nearer the house, continuing on his route. He was taken aback by the weakness of his words, sounding thin in the thin air.

He entered into the heavier woods through the white posts with no gate. It was dark among the trees; it must have been later than he realized. For one instant the sun came out, and it was like being in a cathedral when the high windows let in light and make diamond shapes on the floor. There were crisscrosses of shadows everywhere, thin swords. When they'd visited churches in France, Margaret had always been disturbed by the tombs being set into the ground, unguarded, so people walked over them, polishing down the stone — disrespectful, she said. He could hear the hum of traffic out on the highway and thought of how these woods had once been quiet, only chirping birds and creaking trunks. The path turned and he followed it down an incline and the hum faded. Rather than being satisfied with the difference, it merely highlighted his irritation.

He came out on Welch Road. A black dog ran to the corner barking, and barked there hoarsely as Mr. Eliot went by. He'd seen the dog before, and knew that going by any faster would not make any difference, so he did not hurry. The dog stood with its legs apart, snapping at the air. It did not matter that Mr. Eliot was Mr. Eliot, the dog would have been barking at anyone. As Mr. Eliot went up the hill, he found the slope steeper than usual. A car drove up from behind, idling near him in the twilight, then passing with a little rev.

They were irritating, these cars. His breath came shorter as he continued up the hill. The shadows fell over him. Involuntarily he thought of Harry Sprague dropping on the eighth tee last July at Longwood. Harry Sprague had been younger than Mr. Eliot and, Mr. Eliot had always thought, more fit. He had allowed himself, at his death, the tiniest satisfaction that he'd outlasted him. Harry Sprague had been an old friend and would not have taken offense. His son Charlie had limped up to the podium and had given the eulogy which moved everyone. Mr. Eliot tried to envision Arthur in the role and scoffed at the idea. Arthur was good at smart talk. Mr. Eliot had specifically not named his son after himself with the hope of granting the boy a degree of freedom. He guessed he'd succeeded there.

But what was he thinking of that nonsense for? He was getting a little tired and his brain was going. It was what happened when you got old, at least that's what idiots were always saying. He would take a nap when he got home, and have only a little soup for dinner. All that rich food at lunch was making him sluggish, he shouldn't have let her put on all that yellow sauce.

He achieved the hill.

Past the Wilsons' he noticed a new house which had gone up overnight. Canvas flapped against the skeletal form. The ground was dug up, and leaves had collected in the muddy ditches.

He turned onto Curtis Road, their road. He heard children shouting behind the Stockwells'. In the light they must have been having a touch football game out on the lawn. George Stockwell would be out on the terrace watching, a blanket over his lap, in his wheelchair.

He felt hot. His forehead was wet. Passing under the pines it was cooler, the sun never shone there at all, and then he came to their graveled turn. He stopped for a moment and leaned against the big elm. His heart was pounding in his ears, and he felt rotten. Their sign was there across from him by the rhododendrons, a white sign with E. M. ELIOT painted in black. He noticed for the first time, though he'd seen the sign for years, that the letters had a wave to them as if they were underwater. He blinked. Was his sight going? Could he really not have noticed it properly all this time? He did not feel well at all. He wanted to lie down. He would stretch out on the library sofa till his radio show then go to bed early. Something about those letters unnerved him, seeing his name in unfamiliar print, and as he made his way slowly up to the slender pillars on either side of the front door, he tried to think of what it was. As the light faded around him, he had a growing sense of dread.

He looked behind him suddenly with the peculiar sensation that someone had been following him. The person had been there the whole of his walk, crouched against the tree trunks, hidden by the Olneys' garbage cans, crawling among the Colchesters' rosebushes. A shiver ran through him. He remembered a walk he'd once taken with Arthur a long time before on the Island when Arthur had torn off into the woods and disappeared. He couldn't remember why. At first Mr. Eliot had worried he was lost till he saw the striped sock and bare calf peeking out from behind a mossy rock. So he had played along, ignoring the crackling of twigs and the rustle of leaves. Mr. Eliot did not let on he saw the flash of green jersey back on their road, or the little figure dashing in the back door, he'd walked up to the house slowly, hands loose at his sides, jauntily taking the rise of the lawn. And when he opened the door, Arthur was standing there with a shiny look of surprise on his face, delight lifting the edges of his eyes. Mr. Eliot thought of it now, distraught, it had been such a pleased face. Then there was his own father's face the time he'd broken the ice chest handle, disappointed, and they were getting all mixed up, the bright hopeful face at the door and the adult sour face, admonishing him, judging.

He paused to catch his breath but could only manage a shallow panting. It seemed as if the thing which had been following him had now gone on ahead, sneaking forward as Arthur had done. This time it had gone into the house: it was in the library, it had crawled under the sofa where Mr. Eliot planned to lie down. He did not hurry to it. As he went forward, he could practically hear the panting mouth, expectant, ready to take him.

AFTER MR. ELIOT'S death, Lilian hired a number of nurses to look after Mrs. Eliot. It was hard to keep them straight.

Late one afternoon, one of the nurses telephoned Lilian in a sharp clipped voice, implying with each emphasized word that it was not her fault, she had left her as usual in the living room at four o'clock, and when she came back just ten minutes later the french door was ajar and Mrs. Eliot was gone. Lilian assured her she couldn't have gone far and said she'd be right over. Since Mr. Eliot's death, Lilian had spent a great deal of time in Brookline.

Turning onto Curtis Road, Lilian saw her mother's pale blue sweater ahead in the dusk, heading down the dip toward the Colchesters' pillars. She got out of the car.

Ma, Lilian said. She walked over to the light blue sweater and the white hair. Outside, with the sky dwarfing the two of them, Mrs. Eliot seemed suddenly very small. Her head was upright on her narrow shoulders, but her back had begun to curve over. Lilian felt like a giantess.

Mrs. Eliot frowned, putting out her elbow, to fend off. Who's that? she said.

It's Lilian, Ma.

Mrs. Eliot shook her head. I don't know any Lilians, she said impatiently. Darkness had collected around the trees and Mrs. Eliot's hair stood out like a white handkerchief.

Come back to the house.

You get off my land, said Mrs. Eliot.

Ma.

Mrs. Eliot's eyes showed the whites, a faded custard white, and her arms stiffened akimbo. You people think you can go anywhere. This is private property. She took small steps on the gravel, keeping close to her cane. People, she said with disgust.

This isn't even our driveway, Lilian said absurdly.

I'm going to see Agnes, said Mrs. Eliot.

She's not there, Lilian said.

Mrs. Eliot regarded her with interest.

They're away, Lilian said.

Agnes Colchester had died ten years before of pernicious anemia.

Who's going to cut back the roses? said Mrs. Eliot. Their gardener doesn't do it right. She shrugged, deciding it was their problem after all. I could get Edward to help, I suppose . . .

Come on, Ma. Lilian took her arm. Was this how one ended up? Worrying about roses, visiting the dead . . .

As they walked up the gravel drive, Mrs. Eliot spoke with an ominous tone. Is she there?

Lilian saw a white blur standing behind the narrow window by the door. She was worried about you, she said.

She's a monster, said Mrs. Eliot.

You said you liked her.

Mrs. Eliot pressed her mouth together, refusing to say more.

When they opened the door the nurse was there. She had a mustache and wide ankles in white stockings. Was this the one named Monica?

Next time we take a walk, said the nurse, we take it together.

Lilian expected her mother's long-perfected look of disdain and was surprised to see a contrite childish face nodding in submission.

Since it was difficult for Rosie to climb the stairs, Mrs. Eliot's bed had been set up in a room off the library. She died there in her sleep.

Mr. Eliot's death, so quiet and sudden on that Sunday evening, had so stunned Lilian that her mother's death was like adding a bucket of black paint to an already dark barrel.

Lilian wired Arthur at a dozen addresses and finally got him in Miami. He arrived a day later than he'd said, but in time for the funeral. He'd been there for their father's, delivering the eulogy which he'd cut short with emotion. He had appeared too, at Irene Putnam's the spring before, standing a little longer at the burial while the mourners streamed like ink back to their cars. Lilian had seen him pick up something from the ground, a pebble or a leaf, and pocket it. He looked different each time he came, once wearing a loud tie, another time looking elegant and shady. On this visit he sported a worn-out cashmere jacket, dilapidated shoes, and was badly in need of a haircut. When

Lilian pointed it out he replied that he'd so little hair it hardly mattered.

Lilian and Arthur walked through the house in Brookline discussing what to do with the things. Arthur threw out suspicious glances as he entered doorways, expecting to encounter his father's ghost. Perhaps he did for the look of fright he had about him. Lilian asked him about life in Florida and he said, You can't beat the weather, and discussed it no further. A number of phone calls came for him during his visit, from gravelly voiced men. He was particularly concerned with the arrival and departure times of the post, sending off a number of letters, and anxiously looking through the stack of mail which arrived.

The night after Mrs. Eliot's funeral, Arthur stayed with the Finches on Joy Street. He mixed his second drink after downing the first standing up. Lilian thought of the old Arthur who used to make cakes out of daisy innards and serve them to her on rocks.

The children regarded him warily, not remembering the last time they'd seen their uncle — it had been a number of years before, but within a half hour the girls were climbing on him. He made Fay giggle which was not hard, and Sally laugh which was. Porter stood apart, gazing at him with interest.

After dinner Arthur sat with Gilbert by the fire talking of nothing in particular, using the polite tones of men who share a connection through a woman but, having little else in common, are never destined to be friends. Lilian joined them and they discussed what to do with the furniture and the house. The men had gotten somewhat sloppy by this point and Lilian attributed that to Arthur's suggestion that they auction everything off. She proposed that instead of selling Curtis Road, Lilian and Gilbert and the children would move in and reimburse Arthur for his share. At the mention of payment, Arthur's eyes shrank to a satisfied point and he nodded that it would be just fine with him.

Lilian had the maroon wallpaper taken down from the library and the rugs changed in the hall, but mostly she was too conscious of her parents' absence to want to change much. The ship prints remained in their step formation on the stairway, and the Copley stayed above the mantel where it nicely fit. Gilbert's leather bar with the removable tray established itself in the living room, and Lilian experimented with where to put the Chinese end tables. Her lemon tree did not survive the move.

Now and then she could almost hear her father's booming voice and would shudder with a sort of longing inside, or think she glimpsed her mother's head bowed in her sewing spot. The sound of pearls clicking against the glass top of her dressing table conjured up her mother immediately, and she could nearly smell the sherry.

When the weather turned mild they had a housewarming and set up card tables and chairs out back where a new trellis had been put up for Chinese wisteria. The children ran in circles around the daffodils.

One day as she shut the small drawer of the highboy, the cherry one in the family for years, taking out some of the good matches, Lilian received a shock at the end of her sleeve: she saw her mother's hand.

I HAVEN'T the least idea what you're thinking either, said Gilbert Finch in mild tones. I suppose it has something to do with thoughts being silent.

Just ask and I'll tell you, Lilian said.

I wouldn't dream of it.

They sat at a glass table on the club terrace over-looking the first tee. Lilian wore her blue dress with the white flowers spaced across it, the shoulder pads further straightening her straight shoulders. That night, dressing for dinner, she noticed the wake of grey spraying off from her part. She pinned up her hair and figured that at thirty-nine she could expect a few grey hairs.

Gilbert sipped his drink. If they don't get here soon, I'm leaving, he said.

You know, said Lilian. I don't think they actually introduced us.

Then why are we here?

Well, they played a part.

Gilbert nodded vaguely, this being the sort of thing Lilian kept track of.

I don't think anyone introduced us, she said.

They sat in silence for a while.

But you know Marian, Lilian said. Any excuse for gaieties . . .

Gilbert signaled to the waiter. He fingered a few peanuts from a dish into his palm and ate them one at a time. Presently his drink arrived.

I've never known Dickie Wiggin to be on time, he said.

It's just a drink, Lilian said.

I could be at home minding my own business.

Lilian smiled and patted his arm. The sun glowed from behind the trees. There had been some cool days since the summer, but tonight it was warm again with the dusty smell of leaves. Lilian was wearing her summer shoes. It *is* our anniversary, she said.

Gilbert shook the ice cubes to melt them. Yes, he said. It is.

Oh, here they are, she said. Goodness, Marian looks as if she's dressed for a ball.

The Wiggins approached and engulfed them in rustling organza and crêpe de Chine.

I knew you wouldn't, Marian said. Her hair was swirled into careful curls. I told Lilian to dress!

She looks dressed to me, Gilbert said. He shook hands with Dickie Wiggin and complimented him on his stickpin.

We were hoping we might persuade you to stay for dinner, Dickie Wiggin said.

Sorry, said Gilbert. Tonight it's just me and my bride.

We'll see, said Dickie, winking at Lilian.

They ordered drinks and talked about Cap Sedgwick and the upcoming election.

There's the feeling the common man is not drawn to the Brahmin type, said Gilbert.

But we're not a type, we're not *like* anything, said Marian. Everyone's different, aren't they?

Tell that to the Amorys and the Cunninghams and the Sedgwicks, said Dickie, straightening his cuff link.

Oh, they just think they're that way, Marian said.

Yes, and everyone believes them.

Excuse me a moment, Gilbert murmured. He stood and bowed.

Where are you going? cried Marian with alarm.

Nowhere a lady can follow, he said, backing away.

She shot Dickie a look.

I'll join you, Dickie said, starting up without conviction.

I'm quite fine on my own. Gilbert sped off.

Lilian knew the guise: he would be stopping for a solitary drink at the bar.

Dickie sat down with some uncertainty. Marian shook her head as if to say, it can't be helped.

What's going on, you two? said Lilian.

Marian smiled her merry smile, her eyes slits. We're just happy to be here, she said. Twelve years! And to think we were there! Tell me, how are the children?

But before Lilian could speak Marian gave her a full report on the Wiggin clan. Gilbert did not reappear.

After some time, he came rushing out to the little group on the terrace to tell Lilian that she had a phone call, it was Anna, nothing important, just a question about Porter's ear medicine. Gilbert escorted her back to the front desk which was deserted as always. The phone down at one end of the counter was hung neatly up.

Come along, said Gilbert. We're going.

What?

We are leaving. Going home. He started for the front entranceway.

Gilbert!

He turned back wearily. Your friend has cooked up a reception for us, he spat out. He pointed down the hall toward the dance room. They're sneaking in — I saw the Vernons, and Jane and Jack.

Lilian put her head out the door and saw some fancy people in the parking lot heading toward the side doors. She recognized Emmett Smith and his wife.

Then we can't leave, she said.

Oh yes we can.

They were interrupted by a sheepish-looking Bayard Clark sidling up near the wall with Amy Clark, trying to pass by unnoticed.

You're not supposed to be here, said Amy Clark in her raspy tones.

Neither are you, Gilbert said, and exited down the flagstone path.

Lilian stood for a moment. She went back to the Wiggins who had anxious expressions above their drinks. She picked up her bag.

Gilbert's feeling awful, she said. I'm afraid we've got to go.

But you can't! Marian cried. You don't understand, you see . . . We may as well tell her now, Dickie . . .

We know, Lilian said. It's awfully sweet of you, but . . .

Marian's face was frozen in disbelief.

I told you it wasn't Gilbert's cup, said Dickie Wiggin.

I am sorry, said Lilian.

That's quite all — that is, we understand, said Dickie Wiggin.

Marian was flabbergasted. Why does he have to ruin it for everyone else? she said.

But Lilian was already dashing away.

ONE PARTY Gilbert Finch could not avoid was the victory party for Cap Sedgwick in January at the Copley Plaza. The election had been close, but Cap had had the advantage of being the incumbent. The distant hint of war was felt in the ballroom, making everyone more festive in opposition, and while the talk touched upon Czechoslovakia and Hitler and the shame of the meeting in Warsaw, no one seemed to think they would actually fight again, and their concerns rested on the problems closer to home.

Sitting at a table with a sparse centerpiece of carnations and ferns, Lilian met the people Gilbert worked with. A Miss Berry wearing little wings on her jacket and an orchid corsage on her wrist gushed, Your husband is the politest man I know.

He's a quiet one, said a man named Mr. Noonan, but right on the money. Don't let him fool you, he knows more than the rest of us.

Lilian caught sight of Gilbert across the room, his cheeks with the beginnings of a rosy glow.

Cap Sedgwick mounted the podium to read the speech Gilbert had written. The long Yankee jaw and tilted eyes lent a sympathetic air to his face, not unlike young Abe

Lincoln's, an association not lost on his voters. He wasn't convinced about this New Deal, Cap Sedgwick said, but he would back anything as long as it helped business.

Afterwards a medium-size orchestra played with uncertain enthusiasm, in keeping with the evening's tone. Lilian was sitting before a plate of melting red, white and blue ice cream when Gilbert came to fetch her for a photograph. She smiled up at him and didn't move. Sis Sedgwick, with a barrette in place over one ear and wearing a slim satin dress, said Lilian had to come, they were taking a picture of everyone who'd helped. Lilian protested she'd only copied a few lists and sat at some tables, but Sis had covered her ears not to hear another word.

They were herded together near the ballroom's gold-trimmed pocket doors. Guests of the Copley Plaza milling about in the lobby stopped to satisfy their curiosity about the bright lights. They stood in the door, gaping, smiling to see people being photographed. Behind them were purposeful people on their way somewhere, scribbling notes at the marble front desk, striding off to catch a cab, or returning in pairs for the evening, longing for the elevator. Lilian watched, wishing she were among them. One dark figure passed behind the spectators and glanced in the doorway as one would who had a general interest in his surroundings. Something caught his particular interest, and he walked forward, looking up at the chandelier, and seemed to study the ceiling and plasterwork. He wore an overcoat and a beret: it was Walter Vail.

Lilian immediately looked away, feeling herself color thoroughly. She was terrified she'd catch his eye. What was he doing here? Thank goodness no one was looking, each too concerned with looking right for the photographer. After a few flashes followed by the ash-hiss of the bulb, the group broke up. The people in the doorway moved off. Lilian dared a glance in their direction and with relief saw he was gone.

Dolly Vernon who'd risked an evening dress involving gold cord came up to Lilian, looking tipsy. Come with me to the ladies' room, she said. Since the crisis in the Vernon marriage Dolly had been drinking more, not that anyone would particularly notice, but Lilian had known the particulars. Dolly had met an Englishman on one of their trips to London and nearly left Freddie for him, fortunately coming to her senses in time. It had been the conversation more than anything, Dolly said, blushing despite herself. He could have chatted for hours. Lilian said she wouldn't wish an Englishman on a nice American girl, and Dolly nodded, but disappointment showed around her mouth.

I'll shoot myself if they start up again with 'For He's a Jolly Good Fellow,' Dolly said.

They crossed the lobby. It was Saturday night and humming, the bellboys moving swiftly like robins.

I don't believe it, said Dolly in a matter-of-fact way. She strode over to one of the desks and leaned against the counter nonchalantly in her shiny dress, waiting for the man beside her to stop writing and look up.

Lilian still had the chance to slip away but Dolly Vernon waved her over. She was trapped.

Look who's here, Dolly said. Now I remember — Madelaine told me you were coming — your uncle's wedding, right?

Lilian had not heard about it.

That's right, said Walter Vail. He looked at the women, doing his best to maintain a relaxed expression. Lilian noticed it took an effort and felt glad for that. And what are you two doing here? But, of course, this is where you belong! In the heart of Boston. He did not look at Lilian.

Please, said Dolly Vernon. The Somerset is more like it.

They laughed.

We're celebrating our congressman, said Dolly.

So I see. It was his same voice.

Lilian felt she'd turned into a stick.

Freddie Vernon flapped over carrying Dolly's fur coat with the Wiggins behind, already in their coats. We're off, Freddie said. Marian Wiggin regarded Walter Vail, waiting to be introduced. Lilian muttered introductions in time for them to bid farewell.

Promise you'll call! Dolly shouted as they drifted off.

Your uncle from Lime Street? Lilian said as they walked back toward the ballroom. He stopped with her by the door. She wound the beaded ribbon of her evening bag around a finger.

It's good to see you, he said, with a private tone in his voice.

Her face was implacable.

I don't know if you understood why I . . .

She watched him, she glanced at the palm fronds, she listened.

. . . haven't written to you. I wanted to but I thought . . .

The ribbon twisted through her fingers.

. . . thought it wouldn't have been a good idea . . .

She nodded, unafraid. After the initial shock she was

relieved to be unafraid. She could feel him coming near, and she didn't know what he meant by it, but she wasn't going to fear it. She would simply see. Yes, she said, you were right.

Anyway, he finished, shaking off the apology. I was hoping I would see you.

She looked at him.

You won't believe this, he said, distressed, but I — I was just — He unfolded a crumpled piece of paper from his hand, the telegram form. *Mrs. Gilbert P. Finch,* it said, followed by the Joy Street address.

He did know how to throw her off, but she was determined to stay upright. We live in Brookline now, she said.

Do you?

My family's house. My mother died a year and a half ago . . .

I am sorry, he said. He had a way of putting his face so it seemed as if he genuinely was.

Lilian thrust out her jaw. Much had happened to her since she'd last seen him.

I'd love to come see the house.

She did not like that extra tone in his voice. He had left her twice now, what did he mean by . . . ? No, it was easy to remain hard to him. Nothing he did would matter in the same way. But there was that telegram unnerving her . . . For some reason she thought that saying no to him would be admitting he still had power over her.

Call me, she said with a shrug, feeling she gave a pretty good impression of not caring in the least.

* * *

So that was the famous Walter Vail, said Gilbert. I expected Valentino.

It surprised her he even remembered Walter Vail. They were in the car, Lilian driving home as she always did after parties.

He has his points, she said. It was what she might have said about any other man and she wasn't going to make an exception in this case. She would like not to make any more exceptions for Walter Vail.

Gilbert, usually tired and nodding on these drives, was chatting in a slow way about the rare sighting of a Ross's goose by Chip Cunningham out in Ipswich. Lilian's thoughts drifted back to the day on the Island, not that she cared to moon over her time with Walter Vail, she'd gone over that enough as it was, but seeing him had reminded her — Gilbert was saying something about the soft bill of a woodcock — and she wanted simply to test his influence on her now. Bits and pieces of the time appeared, floating up out of the dark, the sweater he'd left on the porch railing, the way the wind had died that afternoon, the walk they'd taken in the pines after anchoring by Babbage's and the ridiculous talk they'd had about mushrooms. She'd pointed out the famous doorway in front of the Lowes' house, walking home, and then the kiss under the dark leaves . . .

Watch out, Lily! Gilbert said.

Oh, I didn't see . . .

She felt Walter Vail descending on her, looking at her the way a doctor would, checking for any indication of past illness, any sign of lingering fever. She would make sure he did not see anything. She would not waste herself again on him.

As they came into the driveway on the frozen gravel she remembered the tightening of his hand when he said goodnight and despite herself she tightened around the memory of it, telling herself she had to dispose of it, but instead of snuffing it out, she stuffed it away. She opened an old door and put it there.

S HE HAD NO intention of letting him visit. If he telephoned she could make an excuse. But he didn't ring
up, he thumped the brass knocker.

His face as the door opened was apologetic. Walter Vail
knew how to put himself on the right footing. I thought
you might not let me, he said. So I just came.

Lilian found herself in the unusual position of putting
him at ease. She had on her walking coat and was, she told
him, just going out.

Oh, then I — He turned as if hearing a terrible shriek
then wheeled back around. Let me come?

She was motoring out to Concord where there was a
good nursery. She never sent the gardener, not trusting
him with the flowering plants, and besides, there was nothing like walking into a huge greenhouse with its humid
smell of earth and petals and leaves. Why not let Walter
Vail come? What did it matter?

Though she drove, it was Walter Vail who gave off the
aura, as he always had, of leading her, of having arranged
the world this way as a spectacle for her — the snow on the
ground in shallow hammocks off Route 2, the light and
shadow sharp on the snow, the chalky roads. It was a stark

world. They spoke of Hawthorne, trying to recall the name of the cemetery where he was buried with Emerson, Thoreau, and Alcott. Lilian remembered where it was, having visited with Jane Olney one fall. They'd come upon a group of boys from a nearby prep school smoking behind a tomb. Sleepy Hollow, that was it.

They came into town at the end of Main Street, the picket fences up close to the square Colonial houses, the white church spire shooting up. The town was quiet, Tuesday afternoon, with little signs of life, an old woman shaped like a C on the sidewalk, and farther down, coming out of a bakery, a younger woman with a child, both of them eating rum drops. It was a town of solitary women, and normally Lilian would have been one of them.

At Magneson's they walked down the gravel aisles and Walter Vail strolled off as Lilian picked out geraniums with small leaves and bud clusters and chose a shorter palm over a larger for its stem. The man in the oilskin apron referred to Walter Vail as her husband. *Your husband said you wanted hyacinth bulbs,* it gave her a peculiar feeling.

Instead of taking a right when they drove back to the roundabout by the church, Lilian turned left, past the inn and headed, at Walter Vail's urging, to Sleepy Hollow. The high iron gate was chained shut, but there was enough space to walk through, so they parked the car on the road. Lilian took off her overcoat and lay it over the flowers in the back.

Won't you be cold? he said, though she wore a jacket underneath.

I hardly feel it, she said. Besides, they'll die, I won't. And indeed she felt nothing whatsoever in the still air.

They walked up the winding road to the hill where the famous graves were, their breath flagging across their faces. They discussed Hawthorne's desire to get away from his heritage in Salem, and agreed that Concord was not so terribly far away in place, though it had been in spirit.

The headstone was a dark misshapen thing, a roundish rock. Walter Vail circled it, pensive. His overcoat was stretched over his large shoulders. Watching him, Lilian felt drawn to him and looked away. She did not want to give credence to that part of herself, but she felt the remembrance of it.

She pretended interest in a row of slim slates with splintered edges. *Shining Mason,* one said, *Sam Pitt.* Out of the corner of her eye, she saw Walter Vail bend his knees and lean forward to the lumpy dark rock and embrace it. A shock ran through her, at the odd grace he managed, at how like him it was to do the odd thing and act as if it were not odd in the least. Did he mean for her to see?

They decided to walk farther up. The sun was low near the tree trunks on the hills, a thick orange band. She said she'd heard he'd been engaged again. No, he said, none of that for me. Doesn't suit me. But he had married . . . ? It seemed the thing to do, he said with the old smile, as if he wasn't sure what he meant. Loved her, I suppose. Yes, she said, then why? He interrupted her. She died, he said. Lilian was flustered, But he had said . . . Oh, it took me another one to find out, but no, it didn't suit me. Doesn't.

Did he — oh, how could she put it? — what then did he hope for? Oh — the bored voice — he hoped to stay out of trouble; he didn't want to hurt people anymore. It was not a pleasant thing to do, was it? Love? she said with a disinterested air. Oh, he shook his head, he was through with that business too, had to be, didn't he?

They walked along the edge of the cemetery, on the rise of a hill.

But marriage suits *you,* he said with a mocking tone.

It's not something I ask myself.

Such a strong girl, he said.

Hardly, she said. He had a way of making a positive thing become something one wouldn't want.

Too strong for me, he said. This surprised her.

She didn't mean to mention it. She'd never complained about Gilbert to anyone before.

. . . the short of it being that he's not been altogether well, she said.

Not much of a life for you, said Walter Vail.

They came to a stone wall which looked out over a valley of tangled trees.

It's the life I chose, she said. Not a bad life.

Isn't it?

He was doing it again, breaking down things, tossing them out as if they'd never had any value to anyone, and making what had seemed wrong look different and right.

And would you choose it now?

She didn't dare look at him. No point in asking, she said and started to shiver.

You are cold, he said. Take my coat.

No, she said. But he had already removed it and placed it around her shoulders It was warm from him. She thought of the sweater he'd left behind, and how they'd never mentioned it. No, she said again, uselessly.

Walter Vail looked out over the treetops. So once you've chosen something you can never change? You can never get out of it? He seemed to be thinking of himself more than of her.

I thought so once. She squared her shoulders. I was wrong.

Always so reasonable, he said.

She shot him a furious look. *Always so reasonable.* For once she did not want to be the reasonable one. She tapped into something different inside. She wanted to learn new things. She was tired of being the one who held things together.

It was some moments later that she extracted herself from his arms.

This was intoxication. Alone later, thinking of him, her body swooned.

She remembered what she'd known before and knew it was here again and as she remembered more a wind seemed to blow through her, and she remembered how bursting one could feel, how filled with life and a sense of the glorious in things, and remembering more she saw without feeling it a cruel side: how rapture had no lasting place in the world, if any place at all, but she ignored that. She had used up great reserves on his account, beating it back, and now with his return her feeling was knocking her over. She did not have the least idea what to do.

Would she go through the same thing again? No, if she did, it would be different. It had to be. A thing cannot be the same each time.

She paused a moment in the greenhouse at home, holding her gloved fingers in a thoughtful pose. She could have sat this way for hours. She was not getting much done.

She understood him better now and herself as well, she would be able to manage this time. How, she was hard-pressed to say, but she felt it. The conviction, never exactly voiced, and therefore never subject to scrutiny, took her back to a familiar old place, full of hope, where she was astonished by him.

He had asked her to come to the Copley. Now, he had said on the drive back from Concord. She had let him drive and the car was full of the feeling between them, as they followed the floating red lights back to town. He was crazy, she couldn't possibly go then, and she was unsure she would ever go at all. It wasn't simple. These were the phrases she spoke to him, but inside something else went on.

She thought of his face and was grateful that it was not triumphant, no, it was worn out and pained. How she loved that in him! She'd noticed a difference that first night at the Copley, the weariness she'd seen in some of the boys who had fought. How many bad things must have happened, she thought, for it to show on someone's face. A lot of life must have crashed up against him. One starts off soft, not delivered into the world shelled over like a walnut — that happened over time.

And could her own heart be wrong if it had been feeling this way for so long?

She stood in the old wing, the chaise in the same place, the glow back in the hearth. What she had known as pain was lifted out of the room and it seemed inevitable that she be back inside.

And he? — she seemed to act as his touchstone, a place he checked in with now and then so he could feel — well, whatever it was she inspired in him. She didn't know.

Perhaps she simply made him feel. But then, she thought, that was not something Walter Vail liked to do for very long.

I NEVER did like the sound of that one, Aunt Tizzy said
with a sly smile. Her voice was more hoarse than usual.
Around her shoulders was a turquoise silk scarf and her
heavy black bangles clanged against the wheelchair arms.
She wore a dressing gown shot through with pink; her
knees behind the fabric were like wooden knobs. Her hair
in the sun was a flame.

No, Lilian said. She looked down, but smiled too.

Difficult men are always more interesting, said Aunt
Tizzy, striking a match.

They were in the sun room, a high-ceilinged hallway in
the Maidstone House in Roxbury, which consisted of an
arrangement of chairs facing three wide windows. Here
Aunt Tizzy could smoke. She held her cigarette with ele-
gance as if to say what does one need a holder for?

Look at Ham Bigelow, one of the most fascinating men
I ever knew — course he couldn't manage even to keep a
luncheon engagement — but he was one of those men determined to destroy himself, which he did — and all those
women at his feet! Put a bullet in his mouth. Poor Winnie
did try, but you can't save someone like that. Winnie was
an old girlfriend of your father's actually . . . I was thinking

of your father the other day. You know, I don't think he ever strayed. Aunt Tizzy seemed amazed by this. But I'm not so sure about your mother.

Ma? It was the most absurd idea Lilian could conceive of.

Aunt Tizzy shrugged, and her glance drifted sideways.

How are the hips today? Lilian said.

Misery.

Is there anything I might — ?

She waved away the question. Tell me more about this young man. What will you do with him?

Why, nothing, Lilian said.

Aunt Tizzy tapped her cigarette and the smoke rose into the pane-crossed sunlight. Outside, the snow dripped, leaving dark streaks down the side of the building. Down the hall a heater clanked, and something rolled by on wobbly wheels. It was bound to happen sometime, Aunt Tizzy said.

What do you mean?

I've known you all your life, Lilian Eliot.

Lilian flushed.

I just hope it doesn't ruin your life, said Aunt Tizzy. It does some peoples,' you know.

Lilian felt, at that moment, not afraid of ruin. Ruin had an appeal of its own.

I wasn't planning on seeing him, she said.

You weren't. Aunt Tizzy nodded.

No, truly. She'd become so confused she wasn't sure how much of this was a lie.

Go ahead. You might learn something. Aunt Tizzy

frowned at a nurse passing by. Unpleasant woman, she said. And how is Gilbert?

He's spending more time in Washington with Cap. I go down sometimes.

Interesting place, Washington.

It is.

Heard from Arthur?

Oh, not in a while.

Aunt Tizzy nodded as if she had more information. I never could stand Palm Beach, she said.

I worry about him, Lilian said.

Can't be helped, said Aunt Tizzy. Oh, he'll be back. At the end. They always come back. Look at me, she laughed and started to cough.

A man shuffled by in slippers. Not always, the man said, half-turning his face. I didn't.

Lilian looked at Aunt Tizzy.

New here, she whispered, and her eyebrows rose with interest.

When Lilian left, Aunt Tizzy told her to bring the children next time if they wouldn't be scared to death.

Lilian walked out onto a soaked path lined with box hedges. In the mild air she felt far from the world, out here visiting Aunt Tizzy. The day was too warm for January, the gutters running, the birds singing excitedly. Somewhere far off were her children, part of her, but far off, and the two men. She thought of their eyes. Gilbert's pale ones with the kindness in them, and then Walter Vail's dark eyes. She'd never had to strain after Gilbert, he was always there. He sat and waited, the waiting man. He tried like the rest of us to do his best, but . . . no, that wasn't it. She thought of him entering a room, the mild face, the empty expression, and how it had once filled up when he saw her. Then she thought of Walter Vail, how he would enter a doorway, with a glance quick and hard, and saw how he was too full to let anything more in.

She stopped at a curb. For one moment she felt she was not leaning toward either of them and was standing on her own, alone, but not frightened by it. She thought: I could vanish, and no one would know I had gone. One day Aunt Tizzy would be gone, she didn't want to think of it, how everyone kept leaving, one after the other, like the boys marching off. And what if she were the one who left? The thought bloomed inside her. Yes, she could go, she wasn't trapped like Aunt Tizzy, she wasn't asleep like Gilbert, she could do anything if it came to that. She stood and watched the motorcars go by.

At that moment she thought again of Walter Vail.

THERE WAS slush on the streets, her toes were wet in their boots. She had come right away after phoning him from Brookline. It was just before dinner. She had sat through tea with Elsie McDonnell and Marian Wiggin. She had dutifully watched the children eat, banging their heels against their chairs. She had been unable to concentrate on a sentence. Gilbert was coming back that night after dinner so she had told Maureen not to have anything for her, she was going out. As she put on her coat she thought of the pleasant, matter-of-fact tone of Walter Vail on the telephone. He did not seem to have any sense of the significance of what she'd proposed.

She came around the corner from where she'd parked the La Salle onto Copley Square and waited to cross. She kept the thought of Walter Vail a little apart from her where she could observe it without confusion. She marveled at how the time she'd been with him was fixed in her mind — his fingers on the hinge of the head of the brass owl, the rap on the french door windows, his brushing snow from her collar. How amusing that I still remember it so well. How surprising that I call it amusing.

The lobby of the hotel was still — no people in evening dress, no orchestra sounds from the ballroom as there had been the last time, and as there had been long before for the tea dances she'd gone to after the war. The desk clerks paid her no attention. She had never been up in the rooms and didn't know where the elevators were. She came forward tentatively. Ah, there they were. The elevator man nodded his little cube hat. Lilian told him what floor.

She got off and started down the hall. The walls were all light padding, and she felt wet and dark. She noticed the room numbers going the wrong way and turned back. Tearing toward her from down the other end, past the dots of lights and damask wallpaper, was a woman in a fur coat. Behind her at a distance was the more composed figure of a middle-age man, his head reared back with concern. The woman darted into the closing doors which shut just as the man came up. He pressed the button repeatedly, then turned on his heel and went back to his room.

Lilian came to the number she was looking for and rapped. No one answered right away. What if he weren't there? Then there he was.

He stepped back to let her in. It occurred to her she'd never seen him where he'd actually lived, had never seen how his rooms might be arranged, but that wasn't something she could do anything about now.

There were some hard upholstered chairs and a love seat which he stood beside. He didn't kiss her hello, she noticed that. Sit, he said, running his hand over her hair, standing behind her.

I ran into a friend in the lobby, he said. Someone I knew

in Paris. I hope you don't mind — she's coming up for a cocktail.

Lilian turned to see his face.

You're angry with me, he said. She doesn't know a soul here, and I felt — well, she is an old friend.

Then I ought to go, Lilian said.

No, please, said Walter Vail. You mustn't. I mean, I couldn't not ask her up. You see that, don't you?

Lilian said she did, and gazed down at her hands.

I mean to say, how could it matter?

What's that? Lilian looked at him.

Why, your being here.

Lilian stood up.

It was funny about people knowing each other, she thought. It was as if there were different species of people and ones from the same group recognized each other — there was a rapt moment, an exclamation — then set about getting to know each other. But then, after a while, one saw that only bits got recognized, never the whole person, some bits by this person, other bits by that, but one was never completely connected up with another person, one was never altogether recognized, except, she supposed, by oneself.

She's good fun, Walter Vail was saying. He leaned forward, trying to be amusing. She likes women actually. Perhaps she'll take a shine to you.

Lilian blushed. A strange expression on his face made it lopsided, and she saw uncertainty, carelessness, and fear. She'd seen the look before on Arthur. But where she'd felt pity for Arthur, she felt something more unnerving for

Walter Vail. She'd always seen the irresponsible side of him, the cad if that's what one wanted to call it, but it had always wavered in him.

She went to the window. The view was cut off by a brick corner, though in the sliver of blue alleyway she could see it was growing dark. She sat down on the wide sill.

Won't you take off your coat?

Lilian's hands remained in her pockets. What do you want with me, Walter?

He smiled in explanation. Come now, he said. I mean, what's the point? People put too much stock in promises. They're usually lies anyway, aren't they? What do they matter?

They matter to me.

Oh, is that the Bostonian speaking or the Puritan? said Walter Vail, trying for a laugh. Or is it the woman?

He turned to the bottles on the glass table and lifted the ice bucket lid with a blithe air. You know, I don't think you know what a woman is.

Lilian picked up her handbag.

You're not leaving? His face took on the expression of keen sympathy he was always so good at. But he didn't care. Caring was beneath him. He could not have done a better job if someone had dared him not to care.

It was ridiculous to come, she said. I just wanted to —

Well, you made a mistake, said Walter Vail. Lilian seemed to hear the clap of a trap behind her.

She crossed the room. His hand floated up, but even he saw the falseness of the gesture, and let the hand drop. I am sorry, he said. He put the drink down. I don't seem to be able to — but he wasn't interested enough in what it was he couldn't do, and the sentence remained unfinished.

At the door Lilian made her last turn. Good-bye, she said. For that is what she had come to say.

Mrs. Finch, is it? said the clerk in the lobby. A gentleman was asking for you. He was asking if — the clerk began, but Lilian rushed past.

S HE WALKED and walked. She had too much in her to
stop. All those secret thoughts. They were not made to
stand in natural light; exposed, they looked deformed and
pitiful.

She thought of Gilbert, and pictured him buttering his
morning toast, *scratch scratch,* accepting everything that
came along. She felt protected by that. He would not
glimpse her. She would be left alone.

The night went from blue to black. The expectation
she'd had when she was young for something else did not
die in her right away, but on that night it began to fade and
continued to do so gradually. She did not notice its dim-
ming and one day it would simply be gone.

For some reason she thought of Aunt Tizzy and how the
older woman had patted her hand today during their visit,
and not so feebly at that.

So it didn't depend on Walter Vail after all, and it wouldn't
depend on Gilbert either. And yet here she was: entering
the sturdy door in Brookline, coming into the dark hall.
The light in the library was on.

She found Gilbert in his chair, with papers on his lap,
his tie strangling him, and a drink on the table beside.

{ 275 }

You're back, she said.

Gilbert raised his pale tired eyes. The cigar in his mouth prevented him from speaking.

Did you get any dinner?

He removed the cigar. A piece of pie, he said. His movements were slow, perhaps fatigue, perhaps drink.

Not more? Would you like me to see — ?

He shook his head. Everything all right, Lily?

Certainly. Did you see the children?

Sound asleep. He began to go through his papers. Where have you been? he said absently.

In town. Dolly's redone their living room again.

It's after ten, I was worried. His eyes were following the print on the page before him.

I walked a little after dinner — this thaw makes it lovely out.

I hope you weren't alone.

It was on the Hill.

I wondered if you weren't coming home.

She was startled for a moment then saw he didn't mean what she'd thought. Where else would I go?

She went to put her coat away and came back into the room.

I thought this spring I might make a trip to Rome, she said.

I'm not sure I can go.

Then I'll go by myself.

Lucky you, he said. He stood up, and went for another drink.

I could ask Jane, she said.

Yes, be better with someone.

You wouldn't mind?

Why should I mind? Be wonderfully tonic for you.

I've been unfair to you, Gilbert. She saw a dim shadow of worry on his face.

What do you mean exactly?

I've made us unhappy.

I don't think so, Lily. I've found my unhappiness all on my own, he said. You have always been fair and honest with me. I don't have any complaints.

Now at last she could show him he was wrong, and confess it, or could continue the lie and preserve them. Some marriages are built as much on lies as on truths.

You wouldn't complain, would you? was all she said in the end.

It's as I said.

She went over to her desk and noticed that her things were not as she had left them. The girls have been playing in here again, she said absently.

What's that? He was standing at the door, his drink spilling a little, papers under one arm. I'm going up, he said.

Fine, she said dimly. A red coal burned in the grate.

She glanced at her engagement book: a visit to Mrs. Sears tomorrow, tea at Amy Clark's, the luncheon club on Wednesday. The life in store for her would unfold much as the engagement book had it. And one day — she could not know it then — the grandchildren would come, surprising her with their long hair and disheveled clothes, their cheeks smooth like hers, and while she knew young people were always the same — it was the older ones who varied depending on their time — she'd find it hard to recall what youth had been. When she thought of how it had felt to be young it would seem far off, belonging to another person.

She went and sat down in Gilbert's chair, feeling both exhausted and wide awake. There on his little table she saw something which made her sit up: there was a book of matches from the Copley Plaza. He must have picked them up at Cap Sedgwick's victory party the week before. She took them up and remembered the clerk saying there was a gentleman . . . No, it couldn't have been Gilbert. Suddenly, she wasn't so sure.

The solace of a moment earlier, that she would be left alone, that Gilbert's solitude corresponded to her own, vanished.

She had already decided: I'm staying. I don't have to like it, and if you come right down to it, I won't. But at least I won't moon after things. My parents did not raise me to behave like a fool.

She turned out the lights and went to the window, looking past the curtains at the sky. No stars. It was a cloudy night. Really, she thought, feeling quite hollowed out, would the sky look so different anywhere else?

She went up the stairs.

On the landing she stopped and looked back into the shadowy hall. The bell chimed on the standing clock. Then a strange thing happened. She saw her father's face. It was something she would never tell.

Acknowledgments

For their various help in making this book my many thanks go to Sam Lawrence, Camille Hykes, Sarah Burnes, Georges Borchardt, Cindy Klein, Carrie Bell and George Bell, Darryl Pinkney, Betsy Berne, George Minot, Dinah Hubley, Dorothy Gallagher and of course Davis.

As for Ben Sonnenberg, I don't know what I'd do without him.